Threads

Threads

Ami Polonsky

SCHOLASTIC INC.

ISBN 978-1-338-23919-5

12 11 10 9 8 7 6 5 4 3   19 20 21 22

Printed in the U.S.A.   40

First Scholastic printing, September 2017

For Ben and Ella again,
because everything will always be for you

Chapter 1

Yuming

The middle of May

To Whom It May Concern:
Please, we need help! There is pale pink factory, few
hours outside of Beijing, somewhere in Hebei Province.
22 children in here—young boys and girls. Trapped.
Working day and night on purses. Hardly food or rest.
Please if you could help us. I am 13. We have been
kidnapped by Mr. Zhang, and I have no family to help
me. He pays off police. DO NOT CALL POLICE!

Please help!
Yuming Niantu

Chapter 2
July 1st
Evanston, Illinois

Clara

I REST MY cheek against the car window as Dahlia's mom pulls into the parking lot at the mall. I wish I were at home; I have no idea how I let Mom convince me that I should spend the afternoon with my *used-to-be* best friend.

"Whoa, look how crowded it is," Dahlia says enthusiastically from the passenger seat in front of me.

"Everyone's probably trying to escape the heat," her mom says, stopping in front of the main doors to Bellman's department store. "So, it's almost three thirty." She glances at Dahlia and then looks at me in the rearview mirror. I sit up straight. "Should I get you guys at five?"

"Sure, that's fine," I say.

"How about five thirty?" Dahlia asks, opening the door and sliding out.

I sigh quietly.

"All right. Five thirty, right here," Dahlia's mom confirms. She turns her head and gives me a sad little smile as I unbuckle my seat belt. "Try to have fun, sweetie, okay?"

I know she's trying to help, just like Mom was trying to help by persuading me to get out of the house for the afternoon. I wait for her to add something like *That's what Lola would have wanted*, but she doesn't. She just waves and I close the door and join Dahlia on the sidewalk.

It's about a million degrees out. As her mom drives away, Dahlia grabs my arm and pulls me through the automatic glass doors, into Bellman's.

Goose bumps jump out on my bare arms as soon as we walk through the entrance. "God, it's *freezing* in here," Dahlia squeals, hugging herself and rubbing her arms. I've known Dahlia since we were babies. I have no idea why it took me twelve years to figure out how annoying she is.

She spots a display of silky scarves and walks over to them. "These are so awesome!" she calls over her shoulder. I follow her and sigh again as I sift through the scarves.

They're thin and soft, and touching them makes me think of spring. I pick up one with green and turquoise splotches, tie it around my neck, and look in a nearby mirror.

Dahlia pops up in the reflection. "That's so cool!" she practically yells. "You should ask your mom if you could get it!"

"Dahlia, it's, like, eighty dollars," I say, examining the tag. "This is *Bellman's*." And anyway, it's kind of choking me. I loosen it.

"Yeah, everything here is way too expensive. But it's *gorgeous*—see how it brings out the blue in your eyes?"

I study Dahlia in the mirror. I can't remember life before I knew her. Our parents were introduced to one another in a meet-up group for families with adopted kids. But it's not like Dahlia and I need to be best friends forever just because she and my sister were both adopted from China. I mean, where you're born doesn't *mean* anything—obviously. I tug the scarf off quickly.

"Anyway," Dahlia says, "I'm starving. Are you? Do you want to go to the café? Remember those brownies they have? Those are the best."

"Yeah, sure."

Dahlia's always hungry. At least we still have that in common.

We walk through the scarves, past the shoes department and the makeup counters, the sign for Bellman's Spa, and the wallets and purses, to the café at the back of the store. The lady at the counter takes our order and hands us a number to bring to our table.

"So, how are your parents?" Dahlia asks as we sit down, like she's an adult or something.

"They're okay." I want to roll my eyes, but I don't. It's so ridiculous that Dahlia is asking me about them, like she could understand anything about what our lives have been like since May fifteenth. I stare out of the window behind her, into the sunny parking lot. I think about the *nothingness* at home—the huge hole where my sister used to be.

"Hello?" Dahlia waves her hand in front of my face. I look back at her.

Sometimes, especially when I wake up in the middle of the night, the hole gets so big and black and suffocating that I feel like I might slip into it and disappear. Like Lola did.

Dahlia shakes her head. "This must be so hard."

"Uh, yeah," I mumble. A waitress brings over two brownies on fancy little plates, my water, and Dahlia's iced tea. I look past Dahlia again, around the café.

Melanie Sanders, one of Mom's friends, is getting up from a table across the room with another lady. I wonder what she's doing here; she doesn't seem like the Bellman's type. I rest my cheek on my hand and turn my body away so she won't notice me. I don't feel like answering all the typical questions: *How are you feeling, sweetie? How's your mom today? Is she doing okay, back at work so soon? And how about your dad? Does he really have to teach summer school? He deserves a break, you know?*

She and her friend inch past me as I study my brownie. I catch a whiff of heavy perfume and feel like gagging.

"So, let's go to the pool after my mom gets us," Dahlia says, stirring an overflowing spoonful of sugar into her iced tea with a long silver spoon. She takes a bite of brownie.

"Maybe."

"Come on! What else do you have to do?"

"I don't know, I was going to . . ." I don't have an answer ready, and I clear my throat. If Lola were here, she'd be able to come up with the *perfect* excuse.

· 5 ·

"It's, like, one hundred degrees out!" Dahlia goes on. "I bet everyone who's not away at camp will be there." She grins. "I bet Adam will be there."

"I don't like him anymore," I remind Dahlia, even though he *is* kind of cute. "I haven't liked him since the beginning of sixth grade. That was practically a *year* ago." That was when we still thought Lola was in remission, I think, an image of her hospital room at Children's Memorial exploding into my mind. That was before her relapse and the bone marrow transplant and the months and months of doctors that Dahlia wouldn't understand the first thing about.

"Listen, Dahlia," I suddenly say, surprising myself, "I'm gonna go." If Lola were here, she would totally approve.

"What?" Dahlia asks, shocked. "Why? Where?"

I stand up. "I don't know."

Being in Bellman's with Dahlia doesn't feel right. Sitting in Lola's hospital room had felt so unnatural all the time—especially in the spring, with the trees starting to bloom right outside her closed window. But now . . . now *not* being in the hospital room feels wrong.

"My mom's not coming for, like, almost two hours, though," Dahlia says, looking up at me. "What am I supposed to do alone at the mall for that long?"

I shrug.

"But what about me?" Dahlia whines. "You're being so rude! I can't believe you're just leaving me here." She continues talking as I walk toward the exit. I'm almost past the shoes section when

I hear her calling my name. "Clara! I'm sorry. Wait up!"

"God," I mumble under my breath. I don't turn around.

"I'm sorry, Clara! I know this is a hard time for you. Whatever you want! I'll call my mom to come get us now. You can hang out at my house!"

I roll my eyes and glance behind me. A bunch of high school kids pass between Dahlia and me. I duck behind a shoe polish display and count to twenty before peeking around it just in time to see Dahlia race past. "Clara? Where'd you go?"

I dash back toward the café, weaving my way through the purses and wallets until I reach the spa at the far end of the store. There's a leather bench just outside the doors, and I sit down and slide my phone out of my shorts pocket.

Dad picks up right away. "Clara, honey, is everything okay?"

"Yeah, everything's fine," I say. "I'm at the mall with Dahlia. I mean, I *was* with Dahlia. I want to go home."

Dad's quiet for a minute. "I hear you," he finally says. "I'm in the teachers' lounge grading papers and eating a sandwich by myself. I want to go home, too."

I rest my head against the wall and study the fancy lights hanging from the ceiling.

"I can be there in twenty minutes, okay? I just need to finish one quick thing. Can you hold out that long?"

"Definitely," I say, glancing around for Dahlia.

"I'll meet you in front of Brother's Bakery at, let's say, four fifteen? Is Dahlia getting a ride home later?"

"Yeah, her mom is coming in a little bit."

"Okay, Claire-Bear. I'll see you in a few, okay?"

"'Kay. Bye, Dad."

I hang up and look around again. There aren't too many people back here, and I wander around the closest displays of wallets and purses. I pick up a pink-and-green plaid wallet and turn it over in my hands.

"*Claaara?*" I suddenly hear.

I shove the wallet back on the rack and scoot around the display until I'm on the far side, next to a shelf of old-lady purses. I peek between them. I can't see Dahlia anywhere.

"*Claaara?*" Her voice sounds farther away and kind of worried. I feel bad for her, but I don't really have the energy to think about it.

I take a purse off the shelf right next to me and check the time on my phone. Fourteen more minutes. The purse is ugly—shiny and bluish green. The price tag hangs around the stiff handle. $215.00. I almost laugh out loud. Is it lined with diamonds? I think, unzipping it.

Inside the purse are two pockets. I unzip the big one, and glance at my phone for the third time. *A watched pot never boils,* Mom always says. I zip up the pocket.

I have no idea what I'll say to Dahlia if she finds me. If Lola were here, she'd know exactly how to apologize and explain *everything*. I put the purse back next to a bunch of others just like it and imagine my conversation with Dad in the car. *You hid from Dahlia in the purses?* he'll ask, smiling a little, but in a worried sort of way. Right underneath his smile will be a wisp of the black hole that Lola left behind.

I lean around the purses to check for Dahlia, accidentally knocking the bluish-green one to the floor. The purse that was behind it is an ugly yellowish orange. It has a red CLEARANCE sticker on the price tag. I take it off the rack and turn it over to try to find what's wrong with it, but it looks okay to me—aside from being hideous. It reminds me of a dress-up purse I used to play with. With Lola.

I unzip it and try not to check my phone again, but I can't help it. Twelve more minutes and I can make a run for Brother's Bakery.

The inside of the purse is light orange and silky. I can remember sitting on the basement floor with Lola when we were little, cutting green construction paper into strips to use as money for our pretend store. Even though Lola was only a year and a half older than me, she was always completely in charge. *Coins go in this section, Clara,* she'd say, dramatic and bossy. *Dollar bills go in the zippered compartment.*

I smile, thinking of it—thinking of *her*—and I unzip the smaller of the inside pockets. In it are a white piece of paper and a photograph, both folded into neat squares.

Chapter 3

July 1st
Hebei Province, China

Yuming

ALL AROUND ME, the sewing machines *chug, chug, chug* like blood rushing in and out of twenty-one pumping hearts. The sound never stops, and sometimes, when I'm especially tired and my guard slips down, the sound lulls me into a haze. The *chug, chug, chug* becomes the beat of Wai Gong's curved knife as it rustled the yellowed rice stalks in our fields back home; it becomes the rhythm of brushstrokes as Wai Po combed my hair before bed; the *chug, chug, chug* is Bolin's sleepy feet in the mornings, shuffling across cool, clay floors.

But then I snap out of it. I snap out of it and the *chug, chug, chug* is nothing but the sound of the sewing machines—the sound that is the backdrop to this new life.

In our hidden room, someone's always sewing. Even while

others are sleeping on the floor or on the benches, someone's at a machine, hunched over, working extra hours to earn a cot for a night in the sleeping barrack. I've heard the *chug, chug, chug* practically every second since I was brought here in April—in the daytime, the nighttime, when I'm asleep, when I'm awake, because *nothing* has come of my note, nothing at all.

Though I try not to let it, my mind wanders to Wai Po as I untangle the knot of emerald-green thread at the eye of my sewing needle. She would patch my thinning clothes with shaking hands, and when I'd offer to thread a needle for her, she'd shoo me back to my studies. *Work hard, Yuming,* she'd tell me. *Use your brain as well as your heart.* Her sweet face would momentarily turn sour, and I'd know she was thinking of her daughter—my mama, whom I never knew.

I'd nod and say, *I know, Wai Po.*

The sewing machines chug away. I try not to, but I think of Wai Gong and how he would stand in the doorway of our small home to see me off to school every morning, a glass of tea in his calloused hands. *Study hard, Yuming,* he would tell me. *If you remain number one in your class, you will have a different life from this one—a better life.*

I don't want a different life, Wai Gong, I'd tell him, and he'd cough and smile—a wide smile full of missing teeth.

When he wasn't busy planting or harvesting our rice crop, Wai Gong and I would walk to the park, where the old men congregated at stone tables to play *xiangqi*. The old men and me. Wai Gong's friends would smile as we approached, their wrinkles creasing into endless ripples around their mouths. *Yuming,* they would say, *we see you have come to whisper advice to your old Wai Gong again!*

How do you think she got so good at xiangqi to begin with? Wai Gong would ask them, taking out the soft, red bag of circular game pieces that his father had carved from a fallen willow tree. Great-Grandfather had painted the characters on the smooth wooden surfaces—fourteen in rich black, fourteen in gleaming red—and the pieces were heavy and slick with oil from four generations of hands. A few had teeth marks on them, from when I was a baby. Wai Gong told me the marks made our xiangqi set lucky.

I can still hear his husky voice cutting through his old friends' laughter as they'd share his fried peanuts. *Weigh all of your options before you make your move, Yuming. Take your time. Measure the risk before you act.*

I cannot undo the snarl of green thread, so I snap it off the needle, tugging harder than I need to.

Over and over since Mr. Zhang brought me here, I've weighed my options and measured the risk. I followed through on one idea—putting the note in the purse—but six weeks later, nothing has come of it. Since that day in May, I have thought and thought about another way out, but I cannot come up with a plan worth trying; the risk of a beating—or worse—is far too great. Until I can come up with a strategy, I have only one option: to follow Mr. Zhang's orders and try not to slip off into memories. They cloud my mind; this lack of focus would be a disappointment to Wai Po and Wai Gong. My memories make me weak.

I take a stiff emerald-green handle from the table next to me, align it with the edge of the purse on the base of my sewing machine, and begin to attach it. My machine chugs away.

Maybe you could pretend the chug, chug, chugging *is the sound of the birds flying over the fields back home*, I'd told myself when I first got here. In my previous life, I'd return from school to Wai Po's hot meals in the evenings and study late into the night. Then, in the mornings, I'd curse the birds for waking me. Stupid, I chide myself now. I push hard on the foot pedal of my sewing machine, and the stitching splays across the purse strap too fast—sloppy again, like on the day of the note. So stupid not to have always appreciated the birds.

The light is dim in this windowless basement room; I never know the time. I pretend that the three dirty bulbs hanging overhead are miniature spirits watching over me. I've fallen into memories again, into that hazy, uncertain place. It is hard—so hard—to keep my mind from going where it longs to go.

Jing watches from her seat on the bench next to me as I shake my overgrown bangs out of my eyes and look up at the bulbs. I can feel her concerned eyes studying me. Though we can't speak to each another without risking punishment, our proximity in the last row has made her familiar and comforting.

One lightbulb spirit is Wai Po. *Hello, Wai Po. I think of you every day.* One is Wai Gong. *I'm trying, Wai Gong.* And the third—the third is Bolin. *Where are you?* I beg him silently, tears threatening to escape from my eyes. *It's only the two of us now. What will become of our home? Our rice crop? Where did you go?* The bare bulb hangs still in the suffocating air. A fly buzzes around it. It doesn't answer. Bolin *never* answers.

I blink away tears and pick up the seam ripper. I tug at the bright-green threads, thinking back again to the day of the note.

☆

The door to our basement room snapped open and Mr. Zhang entered, as he does every day, to evaluate our work. I had watched him, my stomach churning, as he examined the sewing of the children in the rows in front of mine. I'd hastily attached the amber handle that I was working on; it jutted sideways from the purse like a broken bone, and I swallowed hard, knowing that if he looked closely at my sewing, he would surely notice it.

He paced stiffly up and down the rows, his hands behind his back, grasping his clipboard with pages and pages of order numbers and shipping dates as he peered over the others' shoulders. Even the tiny ones, their clothes dirty and their noses running—some of them smaller even than Min Li, my six-year-old neighbor back home—didn't flinch as Mr. Zhang walked past. They sewed and sewed like always, their bony backs hunched in front of Jing and me.

I stared down at my purse handle. Next to me was the seam ripper, its sharp point glistening in the glow of the lightbulb directly overhead. Mr. Zhang's footsteps approached the last row where Jing and I sat alone on the long bench. If he saw me removing the stitching, he would know for certain about my mistake. If I didn't do anything, he'd *most likely* see the messy row of amber thread and the crooked handle. He'd chastise me for my sloppiness *and* for not correcting my error.

Definite punishment or probable, more severe punishment? I asked myself, weighing my options, thinking of xiangqi. Probable. I pushed down on the foot pedal and concentrated on sewing a straight line. I covered the mistake awkwardly with the palm of my left hand as I worked.

Mr. Zhang was almost behind me, and my heartbeat thumped along with the quick *chug, chug, chug* of my sewing machine. I held my breath. *Keep walking,* I begged silently. *Don't stop here.*

But the footsteps stopped.

Mr. Zhang's arm reached for the purse. I lifted my foot from the pedal and watched the needle stop above the stiff amber handle and wait there. He pulled the purse off the sewing machine and slapped his clipboard down on the table next to me. With his other hand, he reached for the scissors—the extra-sharp ones with the orange handle. He cut my thread, snapping the purse free from the machine. I looked down at my lap and listened to the sound of him turning the purse over and over.

His voice was sharp. *Your work is* sloppy. He spit the words at the back of my head, picking up the seam ripper and yanking out the amber threads with angry tugs. *Start again,* he ordered, shoving the purse back at me. There were tiny holes in the fabric where my crooked stitching had been.

No lunch for this one, he announced to the guard at the other end of the room. Nobody had stopped sewing, but everyone could hear him. *She needs all the time she can get to practice her craft.*

His words made me furious. I was starving. I'd finish each paltry meal only slightly less hungry than when I started it.

I glanced at the clipboard on the wooden table next to me. *I need to get this order to Beijing tonight,* Mr. Zhang grumbled angrily.

I examined the rows of numbers and cities. Most of the *ship from* locations were Beijing. A few were Shanghai. All of the *ship to* were in the United States of America.

Get back to work. Mr. Zhang scowled at me. *Get. To. Work.*

There was a knock on the door behind the guard—a series of six quick taps—and he jumped to open it. Another young guard's nervous face appeared. *Mr. Zhang,* he announced, *there was a small fire in front.*

A what?! Mr. Zhang cried.

I froze, beads of sweat suddenly dotting my forehead. The chugging slowed around me, but nobody looked up from their sewing machines.

Blood pounded in my ears as my eyes frantically searched the basement room, even though I already knew what surrounded me—four cement walls, a low cement ceiling, one filthy bathroom, no windows, and the guarded door.

It has been extinguished, but two employees were injured, and one of the machines is now inoperable.

Mr. Zhang cursed under his breath. *I cannot afford to lose any machines,* he bellowed. He stormed toward the guard and disappeared into the dark factory, slamming the door behind him. The guard stood to lock it.

In his haste, Mr. Zhang had left his clipboard behind. There was a pen attached to it by a string. I hadn't held a pen in over a month.

I picked it up and, glancing at the guard's back, pulled it toward me. It reminded me of the schoolhouse back home; of the dusty chalkboard and the whispering, giggling students; of our solid table where I used to study in the evenings; of all the places I might never see again. The pen felt alive in my hands.

The idea emerged like a bird from an egg; it came to me, fully formed, crystallized, the way the answers often came to me during exams at school. I weighed all my options and measured the risk. As I did so, the *chug, chug, chug* sounded to me like twenty-one panicked heartbeats—too fast. Unsteady. But then there was *my* heart, which felt firm in my chest for the first time since I'd arrived at this prison.

I sneaked a look back at the guard. He was seated again, and picking at his fingernails. The stack of paper on the clipboard was thick, and I flipped through it furtively. There were dozens of pages of numbers, dates, and addresses.

The sounds of the sewing machines that masked the constant grumbling of my belly would surely mask the sound of ripping paper. The guard now had his head tilted back, his eyes shut. The door was still closed.

I took a deep breath and steadied my hands. As quietly as I could, I ripped a large corner off a piece of paper in the middle of Mr. Zhang's stack. I'd torn through some figures, but the other side of the paper was blank. After a quick peek at the backs of the children in front of me and at the guard, whose eyes were still shut, I hunched over the scrap and scribbled a few sentences in English, grateful for the education that Wai Gong had always told me to appreciate. When I was done, I folded the note quickly into a flat square.

Then I hesitated.

In my pocket was my photograph—the one that had been taken two years ago at the "lucky fountain" at Molihua Park. I was eleven at the time; Bolin was sixteen. Wai Gong, Wai Po, and I had accompanied Bolin to Shanghai, where my brother had decided that he was going to find work. When a vendor approached us and offered to take a family photograph, Wai Gong had said, *I think we should do it,* surprising all of us. *After all, this is our lucky fountain now. Bolin will find work near here to help support our family!* So we'd posed beside the water, the wind blowing my hair, and the young man had printed the photo at his stand.

I peered up one last time before slipping it from my pocket, where I'd kept it every day and night since Wai Gong's death. It was wrinkled and tattered, and I ran my fingers over the four smiling faces.

I held my breath as I folded the photograph carefully into a square. I tucked it and my note into the small purse pocket, zipped the pocket closed, and sewed the strap on carefully—*perfectly*—before tossing the purse into the growing, colorful pile at the side of the room.

Jing tapped her fingernails on the wooden bench. My heart jumped into my throat. She had seen! Would she tell? I glanced at her eyes, but they were fixed on her sewing. Then I looked at her hand. She was giving me a thumbs-up.

I couldn't help smiling a little as I breathed again and picked up another amber purse and handle. I had resumed sewing just as Mr. Zhang barged in, startling the guard. I kept my eyes glued to the purse in front of me as he snatched up his clipboard and marched back through the door, slamming it behind him once more.

☆

And now, six weeks later, nothing has come of it. It was a risk that did not pay off. I sacrificed the only photograph in existence of my family. I search my mind for what Wai Gong may have taught me about how to learn from such gambles, but exhaustion is moving in now. It's clouding my mind. I glance over at Jing—at the deep, dark brushstrokes below her eyes—and I wonder once again what time it is. I wonder when Mr. Zhang will burst through the door into our musty prison and tell us that, at last, it's time to sleep.

Chapter 4

July 1st
Evanston, Illinois

Clara

I WALK SLOWLY through the purses and panty hose, the shoes and men's dress shirts, to the door of Bellman's labeled WEST PARKING LOT. Every few steps, I look up to make sure I'm not about to crash into a wall or something, but, mostly, I stare down at the note in my hand. And the photograph—that photograph—it's of Molihua Park. We've *been* there. It's the giant, famous park in Shanghai where a man whose name we never learned found Lola crying in a cardboard box when she was just a few days old.

I tear my eyes away from the water flowing over the stone tiers and examine the family standing to the side of the fountain. It looks like a grandmother, a grandfather, and two kids—a boy and his younger sister. The girl's long hair is blowing in the wind. The family looks happy—like we used to be.

I wonder which one wrote the note, the brother or the sister. Neither of them looks thirteen to me. And trapped in a factory? How could a thirteen-year-old be *trapped* in a factory, anyway? It sounds like something that used to happen in China in the olden days.

I look back at the fountain—the one that Lola and I threw coins into when we were in Shanghai two years ago. They could be in there; *our coins* could have actually been in that fountain when this picture was taken.

I push through the doorway into the blazing heat, cross the street, not looking for Dahlia anymore—not even *caring*—and sit down on a bench outside of Brother's Bakery to wait for Dad. A hot wind blows and I hold tightly to my note and photograph, the backs of my legs on fire against the metal bench. The heat and the familiarity of that park make everything around me blur and boil.

In the hospital, it was always freezing; *everything* was freezing—the chairs, the doorknobs, the bed rails, the trays of gross hospital food. Mom, who was always worried about me and Lola being too cold, even before Lola got sick, would layer blanket upon blanket over Lola's skinny, weak body in the hospital bed until her pale cheeks turned pink. *Help me, Clara,* she'd whisper when Mom wasn't listening, trying to smile. And, with goose bump–covered arms, I'd pull some of the layers away.

A lady pushes a stroller through the shimmery heat in front of me. The revolving door into Brother's Bakery swirls behind me. I read the note again. It almost feels like I'm not really here—like the day nine months ago when Mom and Dad sat me down at the kitchen table and told me that Lola had relapsed.

Lola left us notes to find after she died. Even though they were addressed to me, she *really* left them for Mom and Dad, because I was the one who had to hide them around the house for her. In the hospital, she wrote hundreds of messages on pale-pink paper—things like: *I love you guys. Grandpa Morris and I are playing chess together on a cloud. I'm totally destroying him! Love always, Lola.* She'd pass them to me when Mom and Dad were out in the hall, talking to the doctors in quiet, frantic whispers, and I'd tuck them into my backpack and bring them home.

After she died, when Mom and Dad went to the funeral home to make arrangements, I hid her notes *everywhere*. I pulled books down off shelves and tucked the pink papers between the pages. I put them under Mom and Dad's pillows. I scattered them through their underwear and sock drawers. I stashed them with the silverware, under couch cushions, in the piano bench, under the grill lid, and in the gardening shed. I did it because Lola told me to, and because I wanted to keep her alive for Mom and Dad.

A car horn honks and I snap my head up. Dad is waving to me through the closed window, the air around his car glistening in the heat. I stand up. I don't know what to do with this letter and photograph, but Dad will.

He's scrolling through something on his phone—probably a text from Mom asking him how I'm doing, if I seem like *myself*.

I open the car door and look one more time at Yuming's photograph before getting in. Finding a picture of *this* park in a purse in Bellman's seems way too coincidental not to mean something.

It's almost like, this time, the message is for *me*.

Chapter 5

Yuming

ONE LIGHTBULB IS on in the corner and a thin, solitary figure sews below it. It's probably Xiu Lan, a girl about my age who sits near the front of the room. It must be the middle of the night by now; a while ago, the younger children were ushered off to the sleeping barracks, but only after Mr. Zhang had lined them up, as always.

"What did you do today?" he had hissed, trying to scare them.

"We played and learned!" they had chanted in unison, as they have been taught.

"Did you sew?"

"We are too young to sew!"

He had nodded in approval before shoving them through the narrow doorway.

Jing and I and the older ones lie on the benches and the cold basement floor. I could work extra hours in exchange for a cot in the barracks, but it would take more than the promise of a lice-infested mattress to persuade *me* to sew overtime. Before we know it, Mr. Zhang will burst through the door, startling the sleeping guard. He'll wake us brusquely, standing on tabletops to turn on the rest of the overhead bulbs.

It's in the darkness, with the sound of the sewing machines subdued, that the demons often come to haunt me. I turn onto my back, desperate to find a comfortable position. On the floor next to me, Jing is breathing as if she's still awake even though she hasn't moved. I consider whispering her name. We have exchanged hushed pleasantries during the chaos of transitions— the lining up for lunch, the shuffling for a seat in the cafeteria or a spot on the floor upon which to sleep—but I long for a real conversation. *How long have you been here?* I want to ask her. *Where did you come from? We can't stay here forever, can we?*

But now, in the nearly quiet room, with the night guard not twenty meters away, is not the time. Instead, I pray for sleep. I know that if it doesn't come, the other things will—the ghostly, dark things that seep into my brain like water; the things that make me feel as if I'm drowning.

I try to keep them away by remembering the breezes that rolled over the yellowing fields back home, rustling the rice stalks until they looked like the wild ocean waves I saw two years ago when we visited Shanghai. I think up crazy things, like time-traveling back to my old life. When I'm very drowsy, a lullaby that Wai Po used to sing weaves its way into my ears. Tears burn behind my closed eyelids as I hear her soft, creaky voice. *The moon is bright, the wind is quiet, tree leaves hang over your window* . . .

I block it by thinking, instead, of the amber purse holding my secret—the purse that was loaded onto a plastic cart by a woman with empty-looking eyes six weeks ago.

It's so hard to keep my thoughts in one place. I wonder if I'm going mad.

An image bursts into my mind, and again I shift on the cement floor: Molihua Park, quiet and foggy in the early April morning, three months ago. A group of graceful men and women were practicing Tai Chi in the mist on the far side of the fountain. They arched their arms in unison as sleepy street vendors set up their stands just outside the main gates. None of the vendors were Bolin, of course. Always restless and adventurous, he had left Shanghai a year before, and since then had been traveling from city to city, exploring and working, sending money every few months. He would include a quick note wishing us well, but not a return address. *Never still— just like his father,* Wai Po would grumble when she thought I wasn't listening.

It had been a year since Bolin had worked at a food stand in Molihua Park, but I went there after Wai Gong died, because I didn't know where else to begin looking for him. Perhaps I would find somebody he used to work with who knew of his whereabouts, I'd thought; he made friends wherever he went. I dreaded telling him about Wai Gong. He still didn't know about Wai Po's death, six months before.

I wandered up and down the street in the gray light and asked each vendor as they arranged their goods, *Do you know of a teenager—Niantu Bolin? From Yemo Village in Anhui Province?* But not one of them had even *heard* of my brother, and I didn't know what to do. I drifted back into the park and stood by the fountain looking around, my shoes covered in morning dew.

Weigh your options, Yuming. I sat on a bench to wait for the rest of the merchants to arrive. Surely *someone* would know of him—the teenager from the countryside, with the easy laugh and twinkling eyes, who used to work at a stand on this very street.

I leaned my head back against the stone wall behind the bench, closed my eyes, and waited for the sun to rise completely. I had never been on my own outside of our tiny village. My groggy mind swam with nervousness and exhaustion.

The bench jostled as someone sat down next to me—close to me—and quickly, I sat forward.

Are you looking for a better life? the stranger on the bench asked me softly. I looked at the man—his yellow Windbreaker, his greasy hair. *I can give you a better life.*

Adrenaline surged through my sleepy veins, and I stood to leave, feeling dizzy with shock.

He stood, too.

I turned to walk away, my vision swimming, but he grabbed my arm and pulled me close. I gasped, and he smiled. *I have a very sharp knife in my pocket,* he told me quietly, looking ahead. *Do not make me use it.*

Nothing felt real. This life is not my life, I thought to myself.

The greasy man pushed me along inconspicuously, subtly looking over his shoulder as we walked. Instinctively, I curled my toes into tight knobs, as if trying to grasp the pavement underneath my shoes—as if trying to hold on to the hope of finding Bolin; to Wai Po's and Wai Gong's spirits; to everything that I sensed was about to disappear.

He shoved me easily out of the park and onto a small, rickety bus, its engine running. It was waiting for us. I tried to yank my arm out of his grasp, but he just tightened his grip. The smell of exhaust filled my lungs, threatening to suffocate me. I should have screamed; *why* didn't I scream?

Anyway, that is what you are looking for, no? A better life? He pushed me up the steps.

The bus started moving before the doors swished shut behind me. The dirty faces of two boys peered at me over and around the bus seats. One had a plastic bag stuffed with belongings at his feet. The other had nothing. Like me.

I didn't know what was happening; I didn't know *how* this could be happening. The windows were open, and fog rolled into the bus. The tires bumped over potholes in the narrow road.

Sit down, the man ordered from behind me.

I looked out the window. I did not sit down.

I said, sit down!

Molihua Park grew smaller as the bus gathered speed,

heading away from Shanghai and anybody who might know of Bolin. Panicked, confused, still dizzy, I thought I saw Wai Po and Wai Gong standing together at the archway. Wai Po's silky white hair faded into the low-hanging fog. Wai Gong watched me intently. *Be brave,* his spirit mouthed to me. *You are a clever girl.* Then I watched them both get eaten by the morning mist.

Are you deaf, girl? I looked down at the man's hand on my upper arm. Next to me was an empty seat. And next to it, the wide-open window.

He shoved me onto the seat. The smell of car exhaust billowed through the window as the bus wove through the increasing morning traffic. I weighed my options, measured the risks.

I lunged toward the open window as the man lunged toward me, grabbing me by the hair. I closed my eyes as his fist struck my temple. Stars twinkled in the dark.

When I came to, the city roads had turned to paved highways. They rolled ahead and behind like gray thread as the bus rumbled north.

There was a painful bump on my temple. The man was sitting next to me, talking. Instructing us.

We were to call him Mr. Zhang. He had ventured far from his home to find workers for his factory. *Clearly, nobody cares for you anyway,* he said, waving his hand dismissively. I swallowed hard, running my fingers through my knotted hair, careful to avoid the throbbing lump next to my eye, and looking down at my ratty, mud-covered shoes.

There were rules and lies, all to be memorized.

Older one, he said, turning toward me, *if anyone inquires, you are now fifteen. How old are you?*

Fifteen, I whispered.

Through the window, I watched the hazy countryside slide past. Slowly, fields transformed into hills and hills into mountains. I blinked away tears.

Younger children, he demanded, staring at the other two, *if anyone inquires, you do not work. You were sent to the factory to be with your sibling. You study and play. Repeat it.*

They repeated it.

I squeezed my eyes shut and opened them, expecting to be back home, secure in my bed, Wai Gong asleep, breathing raggedly, in his bed on the other side of the room.

Good, Mr. Zhang muttered, nodding. *Good.*

Don't try to escape, he went on. *Just ask Bo, the small boy who sits closest to the guards,* he said, his words flying fast, like knives. *He'll tell you what happens if you try.* He shook his head from side to side, grinning evilly. *Ask him to show you his* scars.

Once we arrived at the pale-pink factory, we were ushered into a windowless basement room. I looked at the small boy seated next to the guard and saw a pink, knotted line below his cheekbone. I remembered the sharp knife Mr. Zhang said he was carrying in his pocket, and I thought once again of what Wai Gong and Wai Po had taught me. I weighed my options. I measured the risk. I tried to forget about our rice field, in need of harvesting soon. And when Mr. Zhang placed a piece of fabric into my hands, I learned to sew.

Images and sensations tick in the darkness now—the worst ones, the ones I'll never be able to expel from my mind: the September moon, bright outside the window of the clinic in the nearest village to our home; Wai Po's face, pale and hollow; her chest rising, falling, rising, falling, and then still; Wai Gong's body, cool and hard in his bed on the morning of March twenty-seventh, leaving our small, cozy home empty—except for me.

After his burial, my friends from school spoke to me gently. *Yuming?* they asked quietly. *Are you okay?*

"Yuming," whispers a voice I don't recognize. I see bright, unsettling light through my eyelids. "Are you okay?"

I open my eyes and squint. Jing is crouching above me, jostling me awake by my shoulders. Behind her, Mr. Zhang is tugging on the dangling string of the last bulb. The *chug, chug, chugging* has grown louder. Immediately, I long for the haunted darkness that blanketed the room just moments ago.

The little ones file in through the doorway behind the guard and take their places, bleary-eyed, on the benches. Jing stands up and extends her hand toward me. Disoriented, I take it, while an echo of Wai Po's lullaby swirls gently in my mind. Jing's hand is thin, but her grip is stronger than I expected.

Chapter 6

Clara

I FOLLOW DAD into the kitchen. It's just as hot inside as it is outside—maybe even hotter. The windows are open but there's no breeze blowing through, so I turn on the metal fan in the corner and stand in front of it. It clicks and creaks and stuffy air rushes around me.

Dad was quiet the whole way home, chewing on the inside of his cheek like he was thinking—like he did when he listened to the doctors in the hallway outside of Lola's hospital room.

"I swear, that fan makes it even hotter in here," he mumbles, walking across the kitchen and standing next to me anyway. He rubs the stubble on his chin. Then he takes the papers out of his shirt pocket and reads Yuming's note again.

Sweat runs down my back, and it's hard to breathe this humid air. I wonder if this was how Lola felt when she was trapped under piles of blankets in the hospital—trapped by her poisonous blood.

I wish I could just get out, Lola had said to me once, her eyes closed, when it was almost the end.

Dad was sleeping in the chair in the corner of the hospital room, and Mom was whispering with a nurse in the hallway.

What do you mean? I'd asked, trying not to cry.

I imagined lifting her tiny body into the wheelchair by the door and racing her down the hallway when nobody was looking.

I pictured the hospital wall in front of us crumbling, and a magical world appearing—a magical world where nobody good ever died. The land would be Shanghai and Evanston all at once; Mom and Dad would be there, and Lola's birth mother, too, because without her, my sister never would have existed.

I mean get out of this, Lola had said, raking her arm with flaky fingernails. *Get out of this body. I'm trapped.*

Then she went to sleep. I tried to forget about what she'd said as I watched the white scratch lines on her skin fade away.

"Imagine, twenty-two children *trapped* in a factory," Dad says now, sitting down at the kitchen table.

"So what are we going to do?" I ask, shaking off the memory. I envision a giant room like the cafeteria at school, lined with rows and rows of sewing machines on desks, a young kid hunched in front of each one. In my mind, all the girls have the same long, dark, silky hair that Lola had. The thought makes me feel panicky; the note was written *six weeks ago*.

Dad is still rubbing his chin, thinking.

"Dad? What should we do?" I ask again. If this Mr. Zhang kidnapped all these kids, they must be in constant danger.

He chews the inside of his cheek.

"Dad," I say firmly.

He looks at me.

"We better call the police." I pull my phone out of my pocket.

"Or the Chinese consulate?" he asks, as though he's talking to himself. "I actually think the consulate."

"Okay." I open the laptop that's on the kitchen table, slide it in front of him, and watch him Google *Chinese consulate, Chicago*. "How do you know which office to call?" I ask, my leg jiggling as he scrolls through a list of names and phone numbers. "I mean, will someone take care of this right away?"

"Oh, I'm sure," Dad says absently, squinting at the screen, and I know that he's not saying more because of the black hole; sometimes I can tell that it tries to suffocate him and Mom just like it tries to suffocate me. "Honey, have you seen my reading glasses?"

I go to Dad's briefcase, pull out his brown eyeglasses case, and hand it to him. When I sit back down, he squeezes my knee for a second so I'll stop bouncing it. He puts his glasses on and I think immediately of how, once Lola relapsed, he and Mom spent hours every night sitting at this kitchen table, researching acute lymphoblastic leukemia. They'd talked about chemotherapy, side effects, this option, that procedure. Their voices were sometimes soft and whispery, but usually loud and frantic as they argued about risks and options and what was *worth a try*.

Once, in a screaming fit, Mom threw a chair at the wall. *This is not* fair! she had cried, jolting me in my bed upstairs. I look at the dent in the pale-yellow paint next to the window as Dad picks up his cell phone and starts to dial. I Google *China, factory* on my phone. He puts his on speaker and rubs his balding head as he waits on hold. I scroll through the images of factories that come up. None is pink. I read Yuming's note again.

☆

The middle of May

To Whom It May Concern:
Please, we need help! There is pale pink factory, few
hours outside of Beijing, somewhere in Hebei Province.
22 children in here—young boys and girls. Trapped.
Working day and night on purses. Hardly food or rest.
Please if you could help us. I am 13. We have been
kidnapped by Mr. Zhang, and I have no family to help
me. He pays off police. DO NOT CALL POLICE!

Please help!
Yuming Niantu

The phone clicks and a woman with a Chinese accent picks up. "Chinese consulate, Human Rights, Susan Zhau speaking. Can I help you?"

Dad takes the phone off speaker and puts it to his ear as I pick up my picture and note—*Yuming's* picture and note—and Dad tells her what I found in the purse at Bellman's. I bounce both knees as he takes the note from my hand to read it aloud to her. There seems to be a pause on the other end when he finishes. Dad glances at me for a second and shrugs. "And so this young boy appears to have sent out a plea for help," he adds.

I hear Susan Zhau says something to him, something about a "traditional" something-or-other "name."

The girl, Dad mouths to me, tapping the young girl's face in the photograph. I pick it up again. If she's thirteen now, this picture must be pretty old. She only looks ten or maybe eleven.

I study Yuming's face, her black hair blowing in the wind, and picture my sister as a baby, wrapped in a blanket in a tiny cardboard box and left in Molihua Park—*Yuming's park*—on a sunny fall morning. That's all we know about where Lola came from. After being found, she was taken to the nearest orphanage, two hours outside the city, where her age and birthday—October first—were estimated.

Mom and Dad used to tell us the story all the time—they *loved* telling Lola's adoption story. They had tried for years to get pregnant, but for some reason they couldn't. So they saved and saved for an adoption from China. Once they were approved to adopt Lola, they became pregnant with me. They were so happy and, for a minute, they wondered if they should cancel the adoption, but they knew immediately that they couldn't; they couldn't abandon the little girl who was waiting for them halfway around the world.

About seven months later, they flew to Shanghai to pick up Lola, even though Mom's doctor had warned her that she was *cutting it close.* "If you were one week further into this pregnancy, I'd say unequivocally, 'No, you can't go,'" he told her. Whenever Mom told us the story, she'd lower her voice to imitate him, wave her finger back and forth, and sternly say, "unequivocally, 'No.'"

In the hotel, the night before they were scheduled to get Lola, Mom went into labor. I was born in a hospital in Shanghai the next day while, two hours away, Dad held Lola for the first time. There's a picture on the wall in the living room—our first family photo. Mom is cradling me in a blanket, a tube sticking out of my nose, and Dad is holding Lola on his lap. We had to live in Shanghai for a month before I was allowed to fly home.

Susan Zhau's voice interrupts my thoughts. I hear her saying something about Dad's information.

"Al Clay," Dad says. He spells our last name and gives her his contact information. Susan Zhau then says something else that I can't make out. He grabs a pen and piece of paper from the counter and jots down a few notes.

"Okay," Dad says, glancing at me. There's silence on the other end of the phone. "So, uh, that's it, then?" he asks.

Susan Zhau's answer seems quick.

"Well, then, can we request that you keep us updated on the situation? After all, these are twenty-two human lives we're—"

She interrupts with a comment I can't make out.

Dad clears his throat. "All right. Bye," he says, moving the phone away from his ear slowly, and then looking at its screen— at the picture of Lola and me sitting side by side on the edge of her hospital bed. "I believe she hung up on me."

I feel cold inside, kind of like I did this past March, when I was sitting in this very chair and Dad told me there was nothing more the doctors could do for Lola. "So is someone going to *do* something?" I ask him.

"Oh, I'm sure," Dad says. Then he looks down at his hands. "This, ah, Susan Zhau—she said she would."

"But how will we know? I mean, what will she do?"

"I'm supposed to scan and email the note and picture, and then mail the originals to her." He checks the time on his phone. "The post office is just closing. We can send them tomorrow morning. I'll give it a week, and then I'll call her to follow up, okay, honey? We'll keep on it."

"We have to send the real ones?" I ask. "What if they get lost in the mail or something?"

"That would be really unlikely, Claire-Bear," Dad says, closing the computer. "Anyway, that's what this Susan woman said to do." He picks up Yuming's note and photograph and takes them over to the printer in the corner of the kitchen.

"Don't you think we should drop them at the consulate?" I ask, still imagining the rows of kids in the factory. "I mean, this is a huge deal, Dad!"

As the printer slowly scans the photograph and note, the lines on Dad's forehead soften, like the black hole is loosening its grip on him. "Yeah, okay," he agrees. "I have a dentist appointment, but maybe you and Mom can deliver them first thing in the morning."

I nod, relieved.

"I want a copy, too," I say, reaching across and pushing the green button on the printer. I watch the paper slowly pulse out. The photocopied images aren't as crisp as the originals, but I'm glad to have them. I take the paper upstairs to Lola's room.

Her desk is just how she left it, cluttered with art supplies. Nobody has put them away, even though Lola was the only one who used them; she was the only artistic one in the family. I pick up her good scissors—the sharp silver ones with the orange handle—and I cut Yuming's note into the same jagged triangular shape as the original. Then I cut out the copy of the photograph and look at it carefully. In her note, Yuming says she has no family to help her, but in the picture it looks like she's standing with her brother and maybe her grandparents. I wonder what happened to them. Maybe she's an orphan now, like Lola was.

On the bulletin board above Lola's desk is a postcard of the fountain in Molihua Park. We bought it at a stand just outside the park when we visited China two summers ago. I was ten and

Lola was eleven. That was more than a year before her relapse. She had seemed so healthy.

We flew to Beijing and went to all the typical tourist sites before taking an overnight train to Shanghai to visit the park where Lola had been found as a baby. The next day, we took another train out to the countryside and went to her orphanage.

I untack the postcard of the fountain and put it next to Yuming's photograph. I look back and forth between them. There's a semicircle of willow trees behind the fountain in each photograph, and beyond the trees are Shanghai's skyscrapers. Around the low, stone walls of the fountain, silver drains catch the splashing water as it spills over.

I try to envision Lola's face, because sometimes I can still see her clearly in my mind. Other times, even though it's been only six weeks since she died, I just see a foggy blob, and more and more, I only see emptiness—the space where she used to be. When that happens, I know the black hole is coming for me.

When I finally went back to school for the last two weeks of sixth grade, we were studying black holes in science. Mrs. Shannon didn't make me do the work or take the test, but I paid attention anyway, because what she said about black holes made me think of Lola. Black holes are places where nothing exists, but the nothingness is a thing, and that's how it is with Lola.

Lots of times when I'm lying in bed, especially when I'm trying to go back to sleep in the middle of the night, I can feel the black hole seeping out from under Lola's covers, where she's *supposed* to be. It slips across the hall, into my bedroom, and sometimes, I *want* to let it get me, because it would just be easier that way.

Lola's bed is neatly made now, which is annoying, because when she was alive, it never, ever was. Her stuffed animals are lined up against her pale-blue wall—even the ones she didn't care about and never had on her bed before. As I tack Lola's postcard back up, the front door downstairs opens and closes. I hear Mom and Dad talking quietly.

Their voices make me remember those first nights when Lola was back in the hospital, after the relapse that was never supposed to happen. Mom and Dad would stay up late whispering, debating, screaming. I never told Lola about the screaming, even though before that, I had told her *everything*. I didn't want her to worry.

I pull the trundle out from under Lola's bed. I used to sleep on it when we had slumber parties in her room on the weekends. There are no sheets on it anymore, so I lie down on the bare mattress and count while I'm breathing, the way Mom taught me to do: in—*one, two, three*—and out—*one, two, three*. In and out.

Pots and pans clang in the kitchen. I close my eyes. I breathe and count and try to pretend it's before. Before I knew there's a girl in trouble somewhere in China. Before I found a photograph and a letter that feel like secret messages just for me. I try to pretend that when I look up at Lola's bed, she'll be there. It's a Sunday morning, and Mom will come to the door and tell us she's made waffles for breakfast. Lola and I will stumble sleepily down the stairs and eat in our pajamas.

But when I open my eyes, Lola's bed is empty. I try again to picture her on it, but I can't. I pull her little pink crocheted blanket off the foot of her bed and cover myself with it even though it's hot and stuffy in her room.

I study the shadowy ceiling, still breathing in and out carefully—still trying to keep the black hole away. I think about Yuming's park—Lola's park—and the day we visited it two summers ago. Lola and I ate dumplings from a stand, and Mom and Dad held hands as we wandered around. Our family was *perfect*.

I'm counting and trying to relax all of my muscles, but it's not helping. Sometimes *nothing* helps, and I just have to let the black hole wash over me. I want to go get Mom and Dad, but I also don't want to, because I want them to think I'm fine. I listen to snippets of their conversation. "She wants to hand deliver it to the consulate. . . . I just can't believe it. . . . Tell Clara we'll have an early dinner. . . . Will you call the insurance company tomorrow? The hospital keeps sending us the same bill. . . ."

The black hole is lapping at my feet, and there's no point trying to kick it away anymore, so I close my eyes, clench my fists, and let it come for me. . . .

But I'm wrinkling Yuming's note and picture, so I loosen my grip. My hands are shaking. I look at the picture of her family one more time. Yuming kind of reminds me of Lola, the way she's standing with her feet a little apart, like she's ready to fight if she has to. She's smiling sort of how Lola smiled, too, with her mouth closed, like she just heard something funny and is trying not to laugh.

Suddenly, I can breathe again. I sit up. The black hole is gone, like a wave that got sucked back into the ocean.

Looking at Yuming in this photograph makes me feel so calm—calmer than I've felt in six weeks. She probably wants it back, especially if she's an orphan now. Maybe I could somehow get it to her. . . .

An idea comes to me. What if I could find her? Susan Zhau obviously isn't going to do anything. Maybe *I* could somehow get Yuming out of that factory. It sounds crazy, but it might not be *that* crazy—I mean, we're from opposite sides of the world, but we've both been to the same park in Shanghai. . . . Maybe that's a sign that I'm supposed to help her.

I stare at up Lola's bed. Suddenly, I can see my sister there, crystal clear. She's looking down at me, a closed-mouth smile spreading on her healthy face. *Yes!* I imagine her shout, and I want to cry because she seems so *real*.

Obviously, Mom and Dad would think it was dangerous and ridiculous and stupid to try to save Yuming, and maybe it is, but I wouldn't need to tell them my *real* plan. It sounds impossible, but maybe it's not *that* impossible.

I can picture Lola nodding at me encouragingly. Maybe I could do it. . . . Maybe I could come up with a way to get us back to China this summer.

Chapter 7

July 2nd
Hebei Province, China

Yuming

THE POUNDING OF the sewing machines matches the pounding in my head. It *must* be time to eat by now. I tug at the violet thread dangling from the purse I'm working on and glance around for the seam ripper. I'm the only one who constantly needs to use the stupid tool. Next to me, Jing snips a thread carefully with scissors before passing the seam ripper my way. She glances up to the guard and then turns to grin at me, as though she's teasing me for my inability to sew. I almost want to laugh.

The door to our room creaks open. My heart flutters, and I look back down at my sewing. I know very well that by now someone in America could have found my note, and I curse myself yet again for signing my name *and* including the photograph. I wasn't thinking; those risks were unnecessary.

Whoever finds the note could easily notify Mr. Zhang or the police.

I listen to Mr. Zhang talk to the guard—harsh, hushed words, like always. A boy's voice loudly joins their conversation, his words sharp and quick, like tiny punches. "No," he says. "No way. Li, let's go."

I look up to see Mr. Zhang holding a new boy tightly by the arm. The boy appears to be about my age, and next to him is another boy—a clone, only smaller. They are the first new children since my arrival and I bristle, watching them. The little one stands close to his brother, who has a protective hand on his shoulder. "No way," the older one says again, looking the sewing machines over—looking *us* over. "Let's go, Li."

I stop sewing to watch. On one side of me, Jing's machine chugs away, a tense heartbeat among twenty others. As Mr. Zhang drags the boys to the two unused sewing machines beside mine, my own arm prickles. Mr. Zhang shoves both of them onto the empty bench to my left. "Street urchins," Mr. Zhang spits at them. "I see nobody has taught you to respect your elders. *I* will teach you."

I study their faces. "Get to work," Mr. Zhang continues. The younger one looks puzzled. His face is lined with rivers of clean skin where his tears have washed away the grime. The older one's chin juts out in defiance as he glances quickly around the sewing room, as though he's searching for something. His eyes are deep black and intense. They don't focus on any one thing for long.

"I said, get to work," Mr. Zhang repeats harshly. The boys sit there. I look up at Mr. Zhang's face. He's staring at *me*.

I quickly turn back to my sewing machine, pick up the violet purse with its partially attached handle, and slide it under the needle, which I lower into place. Beside me, Mr. Zhang gives the new boys instructions on what to sew, how to sew, when to talk or get up (never), and when to follow his orders (always). I hear him rustling through fabric scraps to find pieces for them to practice on. "In no time, you'll be experts," he says dryly. I remember him saying the same words to me when I arrived. "My wife, Mrs. Zhang, will soon be in to teach you more. For now, you'll practice on your own." He pauses before adding, "And you'll remember. You'll remember what I told you—about the police."

I finish my handle and move on to the next purse. Beside me, the sewing machines gasp, on and off, as the boys struggle to figure out their new lives.

Mr. Zhang leaves, and I look over to see the older boy attempting to guide the fabric scrap under the needle. Even as he shoves it into the machine, his eyes wander the room. I want to get up and teach him what I've learned—how to clear the jumble of threads from the path of the needle, how to thread the needle quickly and efficiently—but the guard is eyeing me, his evil brow crinkled, so I stay put.

Before I resume my sewing, I finger my empty pocket and wish, yet again, for my photograph, the only one of my family that exists in this world. It was my last link to my old life—at least, the last link I could actually hold in my hands. I wonder if the purse traveled to America on a boat or an airplane. Either way, it must have arrived in the United States by now. Maybe a powerful person there has found my cry for help and is coming for me. . . . I pray again that if someone *has* read the note, they won't go to the local police or notify Mr. Zhang.

Jing pokes my thigh under the table and glances quickly to the guard through her long bangs, then back at her sewing. He's watching me with narrowed eyes, and I realize I've been idle too long. Quickly, I press my foot to the pedal and finish attaching the purse handle.

The guard stands, stretches, and yawns. I scowl at him when he looks away. I'm sure he slept in a bed last night, not on a cold cement floor like us—and *he's* the tired one?

"Lunch," he says.

The *chug, chug, chugging* stops immediately, like when Bolin and I were younger and I'd pull the plug of his radio out of the outlet, just to annoy him. All twenty-four of us stand, including the two new boys. Starting with the front row, we file out the door that the guard holds open for us. "Little ones, you enjoyed your studies this morning, no?" he asks—a masked threat.

"Yes, sir," the youngest children say in unison as we walk up the long, narrow, musty staircase to the main floor of the factory.

It's stuffy upstairs, but cooler than in our prison. A few dirty windows let in a foggy light from outside. Women walk about, ignoring us as they push carts of plastic bins filled with purses and clothing. I wonder what lies Mr. Zhang has told them about our presence. What has he bribed or threatened them with to keep them quiet? Whatever it is, it has worked; I've heard whispered rumors that a few of the older children in the basement room have been here for nearly ten years.

We tramp past rows and rows of sewing machines before we come to a stop as Xiu Lan, first in line as usual, reaches the door to the courtyard. "I'm starving," Jing whispers to me over her shoulder, and I nod.

"There better be more food today," I say quietly as we inch forward. My eyes are fixed on the women at their sewing machines, and I don't notice that the others in front of me have stopped until I crash into Jing's bony back. A woman pushing a cart of empty bins appears to be watching, but it's like she doesn't even see us. Instead, she seems to be looking inward—maybe to her village somewhere? To her family, far away? Her eyes look empty and, instinctively, I reach up and rub my own. I think of all the days I've spent at my sewing machine, seeing fabric and thread and, beyond them, in wavy shadows of memory and longing, my home. Wai Po and Wai Gong. Bolin. I wonder how dead *my* eyes look. I know of no mirrors in this factory.

The line moves forward again, and soon we are in the courtyard. The air outside is cool today—almost cold—and goose bumps pop out on my body. I raise my arms to feel what little wind is able to roll over the tall, pale-pink walls, and I lean my head back to look up at the hazy white sky. Clotheslines, crowded with stiff, drab garments, stretch overhead. Beyond the back wall, what I believe to be Cangyan Mountain is visible, and

I stare at it while the orderly line of children becomes a jumbled clump, just like my stitching on the day I wrote the note, six weeks ago.

Our schoolteacher, Mr. Chen, was from Beijing. He told us about the mountains, jagged and harsh, and showed us photographs of the Great Wall of China. The Wall must be somewhere nearby. If only I could get to the other side of these factory walls. But they're like my own Great Wall—impossible to cross.

I follow the others across the courtyard and into the cafeteria. Behind me are the two new boys, hanging back. This time, Jing and I are not the last ones to make it through the dusty, barren courtyard and into the metal-framed doorway.

The cafeteria is empty, as always, except for the guard, the cook, and us. We eat after the workers from the front of the factory. It's obvious that we eat last, because there's hardly ever any food left.

I slide onto the bench of the table near the end, next to Jing and across from two small boys. One of them was on the bus from Shanghai with me. Neither ever says a word. They both stare down at their plates of pasty-white steamed buns and the scrapings of egg—clearly from the bottom of the pot—before they begin shoveling the food quickly into their mouths.

"No speaking!" the guard reminds us harshly from across the room as the new boys sit at the end of the table, the smaller one next to me. They make me think of Hai and Han back home—identical twins. I smile to myself, remembering how they'd try to trick Mr. Chen by switching seats in school.

I imagine them doing the same thing now, but then realize that it's summer holiday. I haven't seen them since April. I swallow hard, thinking of our rice field and wondering if any of the neighbors is harvesting it for me. Life back home is racing forward without me—like the bus that I took to Shanghai in search of information about Bolin. I've been left behind in a roar, in a billowing cloud of dust.

Mrs. Chan plops two plates of food and two pairs of chopsticks on the table in front of the new boys. The smaller boy's plate is missing a bun. "Nobody told me we needed two more meals today. We've run out," she says stiffly before walking away. I look back at the new boys, wondering if they're thinking the same thing as me—that Mrs. Chan must know that Mr. Zhang has us all working in the basement, and that he must be bribing her or threatening her with *something*.

The older boy searches the cafeteria with his darting eyes before swallowing his crusty egg in one gulp. I glance over at the guard, who is standing near the doorway to the kitchen, hands clasped behind his back, talking to Mrs. Chan. Then I turn back to my food.

"How will we get out?" I hear the younger boy whisper to his brother.

All at once, my heart is flooding; a memory of Wai Gong's tan, wrinkled face blooms before me. He nods at me encouragingly across a xiangqi board in the park, willow branches dangling against the white sky behind him. My heartbeat quickens, but I don't look up.

"Shh," the older brother demands.

Wai Gong would playfully shush his friends at the xiangqi table and smile at me when it was my turn, as though he trusted that I was about to make a clever move—even before *I* knew what I was going to do.

"But, Kai, where will we go?" the younger one goes on in a whisper.

I glance up to see the older brother bring his finger to his lips. For a moment, he looks past his younger brother to me. His eyes are sharp and dancing.

As I pick up my pasty bun and break it in half, the image of Wai Gong's wrinkled face winks at me. I slide the bigger piece into the smaller boy's hands just as his brother answers him in a whisper that is nearly inaudible.

"Anywhere."

Chapter 8
July 2nd
Evanston, Illinois

Clara

WHEN I COME down to the kitchen the next morning, Mom is standing at the desk in her sweatpants, holding Yuming's note in her hand. "Hey, Mom," I say, and she jumps a little.

"You startled me," she says before kissing the top of my head. "I could barely sleep last night. I couldn't stop thinking about how unbelievable it is that you found this." She picks up the original photograph from the counter and tucks it and the note into her purse. "I mean, that poor child—children. Twenty-two of them!"

"I know," I say, remembering how calm I had felt when the idea to go back to China came to me. I search my brain for some way to convince her and Dad that we should go, but I have no clue how I'm going to do it.

"Anyway," Mom continues, "I think we should leave right away if you still want to hand deliver these to the consulate. Remember how long the lines can be?" She pulls my flip-flops out from under the kitchen table, and I slide them on.

We all had to go to the consulate to get visas before our trip to China two years ago. Lola had rolled her eyes and sprawled across the black plastic seats in the waiting area as Mom and Dad stood in line across the room. *I'm so bored!* Lola had moaned as I swung my legs in the seat next to her and wrapped her long hair around my fingers.

A strict man had walked over to us, frowning. *You may not conduct yourself in such this manner here,* he scolded Lola in poor English. I was mortified, but Lola just sat up and apologized before grinning at me slyly; she never got embarrassed about that kind of thing.

"Clara?" Mom asks now.

"Yeah, okay, I'm coming," I pat my shorts pocket, where I'm carrying the copies of Yuming's note and photograph. Just having them makes me feel better, and I picture my sister walking into the kitchen in her navy sweatpants and Minnie Mouse T-shirt, her long black hair pulled into a low ponytail. *Don't get too relaxed,* she would say to me. *What's your plan? How are you going to convince them to go back to China, Claire-Bear?*

Mom holds the door open for me and I follow her out to the driveway, glancing over my shoulder at the spot where I imagined my sister was standing.

Lola was always better than me at coming up with creative ideas. If she were in my shoes, she would probably already have five different strategies for how to persuade Mom and Dad.

I get in the car with Mom and picture Lola leaning forward from the backseat. *What are you waiting for?* she'd be saying. *Feel her out!*

I clear my throat. "So, finding that note and the picture—it made me think of China. I hadn't really thought much about our trip there until yesterday."

"Yeah," Mom says, glancing over at me. "Me, too. I can't believe that was two years ago this summer."

I shift in my seat so I can reach my hand into my pocket and touch Yuming's note and picture.

"You looking for something?" Mom asks.

"Oh, yeah," I say quickly. "Just seeing if I brought my phone."

I picture Lola grinning at me from the backseat, shaking her head. I'm such a terrible liar.

We drive for a while in silence as I try to brainstorm, but all I can come up with are the reasons why she and Dad will *definitely* say we can't go: it's too soon after Lola's death; we just got back to work; it's too expensive. . . . I lean back and close my eyes.

Great work, I imagine Lola saying sarcastically, slumping in her seat.

When we went to China two years ago, Mom and Dad had spent the entire year beforehand saving money and planning the trip. Lola and I had counted down the days for months and months. The truth is, I don't even know if they could afford a trip to China right now. And, even if they could, I don't think it's *possible* to get a flight to China so quickly.

You could research the flights yourself, dummy, I imagine Lola saying to me. I open my eyes as Mom merges onto the highway and smile to myself.

☆

The consulate is crowded, just like last time. Mom and I stand in line for a number and then sit down on the hard black plastic seats to wait. The electronic sign on the wall reads 57, and we're number 70.

Mom gives me the originals of Yuming's note and photo to hold. She has a book open in her lap, but I can tell she's not reading. I bet the black hole is sitting right on the other side of her. I concentrate on the photograph—on the white creases where it was folded, on the fountain. . . .

The electronic sign reads 61 already. The line is moving faster than I expected, which should make me happy, but actually makes me feel jittery.

Yuming's photograph looks like it went through a lot even before it traveled to the United States in a purse. The edges are worn and white, and there are little creases all over it, as if it was kept in a backpack instead of a frame.

Mom leans over and studies the picture, too.

"Mom," I ask, "do you really think someone will save them?"

"I do," she replies quickly, but I can't tell if she believes it or she's just trying to humor me.

After Lola's relapse, when we found out that she needed a bone marrow transplant, I begged Mom and Dad to let me get tested; I wanted to be her donor. They explained to me over and over again how it worked—that they had already found a donor of Chinese ancestry; that I most likely wouldn't have been a match for Lola anyway, because of our different backgrounds. But I wanted to be; I wanted *my* bone marrow to save her. At least Mom and Dad could've let me get *tested*.

I glance up at the electronic sign on the wall and then back at Yuming's face. It's almost our turn. I wonder for the millionth time why she said in her note that she has no family to help her if she's standing with people who look like her grandparents and brother.

Mom squeezes my hand. "We're next," she says. I look at the sign just as it switches to 70.

With my eyes fixed on Yuming's smile, Mom and I walk up to the counter. I hold tightly to the papers as Mom asks for Susan Zhau. A minute later, quick footsteps approach.

"I am Susan Zhau. How can I help you?"

I look up. She is younger than I expected, but unsmiling, just like I thought she'd be. She pushes up her glasses and waits for Mom to say something.

Mom clears her throat. "I believe you spoke to my husband yesterday about a note and photograph that my daughter found in a purse at the mall? Al Clay?"

"Yes," she replies without hesitation.

"So"—Mom ignores her rudeness—"we brought the originals in."

"I told your husband to mail them. I have already received the scanned copies."

Mom shifts her purse on her shoulder. "Well," she goes on, like she's not quite sure how to respond, "anyway, here we are. And we brought them." She nods at me, and for the last time I glance at the photograph that Yuming's hands touched, at the words that her hand wrote. Then I look up at Susan Zhau. Her expression makes it seem as though we interrupted her *right* when she was in the middle of dealing with something way more important.

She reaches out her hand, but I don't want to give her the note and picture.

"Clara?" Mom prods.

You have the copies, I imagine Lola calling out from the black plastic chairs to our right. *Anyway,* I can picture her saying, jumping up and running over to me, *this is just more proof that you need to talk Mom and Dad into going to China. And soon.* She'd roll her eyes at Susan Zhau. *Look at her—she doesn't even care!*

"Clara, honey?"

I put the originals on the counter. Susan Zhau swipes them up without even looking at them. "It would have been easier for you to mail them."

"Well, we, ah, we just wanted to be sure—"

"Is there anything else?" she asks.

"Ah, no," Mom says. "Thank you." She puts her arm around my shoulder and gently pulls me away.

I imagine Lola following us, making a *gag me* gesture.

"She's so rude," I whisper as we walk toward the elevators.

"Definitely not the friendliest person I've ever met," Mom agrees. "But I'm sure she'll take care of it."

It doesn't sound like Mom believes what she's saying. I picture Lola getting into the elevator with us, mouthing to me, *There's no way*.

☆

Back home, I grab the laptop off the counter. "I'll be in my room," I tell Mom. I close my door, sit on my bed with the computer, and pull out my copy of Yuming's note to read it again.

It says she's a few hours from Beijing, in Hebei Province. I search for that first, because I can never keep track of where any of the provinces are, and I study the first map that pops up. Beijing is surrounded by Hebei Province, and I look at the area around the city.

A few hours outside of Beijing, the note says. North of the city, I see mountain ranges, jagged lines that represent the Great Wall, and some smaller cities and villages. To the east of Beijing is the Yellow Sea, and to the west and south are more little towns. There's nothing that indicates where a pale-pink factory would be. Obviously.

I go to a travel website Dad showed me once. It was a couple of weeks before Lola died, when he was arranging Grandma Betty's flight in from Minneapolis. I knew he was trying to distract me from what was going on, and partly I was grateful, but partly I felt like a baby for needing to be distracted.

I type in information for flights from Chicago to Beijing, leaving this week. I check the box that says MY DATES ARE FLEXIBLE, and carefully pull Yuming's photograph out of my pocket as the computer searches. I scan the flights as they pop up and swallow hard. Almost six thousand dollars per ticket for a flight leaving Tuesday; four thousand per ticket for one leaving tomorrow. I have to look down at Yuming's face so I don't start to cry. Mom and Dad could never pay that much for *anything*.

"Clara, come have something to eat," Mom calls from the kitchen.

"'Kay."

I click on a tab to sort the flights from least to most expensive and hold my breath as the information rearranges itself. A flight for $575 per person appears at the top of the screen. Underneath it, it says, $1,725 TOTAL. Compared to all the others, $1,725 doesn't seem so bad. I click on the flight and examine the details.

"Clara?"

"Coming!" I can smell pancakes cooking, but I'm not hungry.

It's a ton of money, but nowhere near what the other flights cost. I look at the departure date and time: this Wednesday, at 10:20 PM. My heart leaps into my throat. Wednesday? Just a few days from now? It seems too good to be true and impossible at the same time.

I lie back on my bed and stare at the ceiling. Then I hold up Yuming's photograph. *I'm trying,* I say to her in my mind. I don't know how I'm going to do this, but I need to figure it out. And fast. I tuck the photograph and note carefully back into my pocket and go downstairs.

Dad is sitting at the kitchen table drinking his coffee while Mom slides some pancakes onto a plate. "Hey there, honey," Dad says as I sit down next to him, across from Lola's empty chair. Mom goes back to the stove to flip the pancakes in what suddenly seems like a pathetic attempt to make us feel like a normal family again.

I take a deep breath. The image of Lola nods at me encouragingly from the kitchen doorway.

"So, uh, how's it going at work?" I ask Mom's back.

She looks over her shoulder, surprised. "It's okay, sweetie. You know, Caryn took over so much of the fund-raising while I was away. I'm just easing back into it." She brings the pancakes to the table and sits down.

"Did you finish the newsletter?" Dad asks, lifting a pancake onto his plate.

"Not yet," Mom says, studying her coffee. "I can't concentrate." Then she nods, like she's trying to convince herself of something. "But everyone has been really helpful."

"Maybe you need a break," I tell her. I picture Lola grinning at me.

"I do," she says, smiling. "I definitely do. But you know, with all the time I've already taken off since . . ." She clears her throat. "Well, ah, this isn't the right time for a break."

I look down at my empty plate. *Keep trying!* Lola's image pleads. *Four days! You only have four days!* But I don't know what to say. I have no idea how I'm going to convince Mom and Dad that we should go to China. And *this week*? It suddenly seems completely ridiculous. Mom is back at work. Dad is teaching summer school. And we don't have the money. Plus, even if we did, four days to get ready to go to the other side of the *world*? The whole idea is absurd.

But what do you have to lose? I imagine Lola saying frantically. I can picture her bouncing up and down.

"So, I was thinking—" I say, tears suddenly sliding down my face.

Baby, I hear Lola say.

I look around the kitchen. Her image is gone.

"I was thinking that we should go to China."

Mom puts her fork down. Dad swallows quickly and stares at me. Suddenly, I can't stand the thought of hearing their response. Of course they're going to say no—and then what? The black hole will come. It will choke me and suffocate me; it will *kill* me.

Mom and Dad look at each other, then back at me. I need to get out of the house. This is never going to happen. "I'm gonna walk down to the park," I say, wiping my eyes. "I feel like getting out."

Mom and Dad don't say anything as I grab my backpack and leave through the kitchen door. I can't stop crying. *I don't know how to do this!* I scream to Lola in my mind.

I walk toward the park where Lola and I always used to play when we were little. I'm sure Mom and Dad are watching from the window. I feel like a toddler. I stop at the end of the block near the bus stop, across from the park. Three little kids are playing on the jungle gym while their dads sit and talk on a bench. In a minute, Mom and Dad will probably run up behind me, put their arms around me, and explain with sad faces why there's no way we can go to China on such short notice. I can't bear the thought.

I watch the bus rumble down the street, toward the stop. I recognize the driver: Charles. This is the bus we took back and forth from the hospital once we knew Lola wasn't coming home again. He pulls up and opens the doors.

"Good morning," he says brightly. "Clara, right? Haven't seen you in a while. You going to the hospital?"

I guess I am. I nod and climb the steps, then pull out my bus pass.

"No parents today?" he asks as I swipe the pass.

"Just me." I try to smile at him.

"Okay. Just so long as you're not getting me into trouble." His words make me nervous, but I can see from his face that he's teasing. "Take a seat."

I sit right behind him. The bus is almost empty. Mom and Dad are going to kill me, but I don't really care. I take out my phone, put it on vibrate, and shove it into my backpack. Then I unfold Yuming's photograph and tell her again, *I'll figure it out. I have to.* I lean my head back and squeeze my eyes shut to try to keep the tears inside.

Twenty minutes later, we're in the city. The bus stop is only half a block from the hospital. "Thanks, Charles," I say, standing up and inching toward the steps.

The doors swish open. "My pleasure, Clara," Charles says. "Say hi to your folks."

I nod, get off the bus, and walk slowly to the hospital. It smells so familiar inside the lobby. I pass the gray-and-navy couches, the fake plants, the front desk, and head over to the south elevators without checking in. I don't even know why I'm here. I ride up to the third floor, Oncology, and step out of the elevator.

On the opposite wall is the same mural I saw every single day for months and months. Lola's orange handprint is on it, along with every other kid's who has stayed on this floor. I wonder how many of them got to go home, and how many of them died here—like Lola did.

Sherry, one of the nurses who took care of Lola, starts to walk past, her nose buried in someone's chart. Then she glances up and sort of jumps when she sees me. I guess I must look ridiculous, standing in the middle of the hallway holding a photograph of a Chinese family and trying not to cry.

"Clara, honey," Sherry says, looking around—probably for Mom and Dad—and then wrapping her arms around me.

After hugging me she studies my face intently. "What are you doing here?"

I shrug and she leads me over to the bench across from the nurse's station. Right down the hall is the room that was Lola's. The whole time she was here, there wasn't a thing I could do for her other than pull the extra blankets off when Mom wasn't looking and put her stupid pink notes into my backpack. I couldn't donate bone marrow; I couldn't make her comfortable; at the very end, I couldn't even make her smile.

Two nurses I don't recognize give me sad looks and then go back to their computer screens. Machines beep and buzz, and being back in this hallway with its bright fluorescent lights and smell of rubbing alcohol is making me dizzy. Marisol, another one of the nurses who took care of Lola, comes around the corner, pushing an empty wheelchair. When she sees me, she gasps, rushes over, and gives me a hug. "Clara! Nice to see you! Are your parents with you?"

I shake my head.

"Oh," says Marisol. Then: "Do they know you're here?"

I shrug again, and I can't hold back the tears anymore.

Sherry tucks my hair behind my ears. "Let me get you some apple juice," she says. "Don't move."

"She's not going anywhere. I've got her," Marisol says, patting my knee affectionately. She hands me a box of Kleenex. I notice that she's looking down at the photograph in my hand, and I shove it into my pocket.

Sherry comes back and gives me a little plastic cup of apple juice with a foil top. I don't want it. It's what I used to drink here all the time, and it reminds me of Lola's room: of the tubes and machines, of her tiny body and—

"Why don't we call your parents?" Sherry says gently.

I study the top of the apple juice and nod. I'm sure Mom and Dad are wondering why I've been gone so long without calling. They'll freak when they find out where I am. I may as well get it over with. I take my phone out of my backpack. There is a missed call from Mom, and a text from Dad: *Coming home soon?*

I text him back.

☆

Half an hour later, the elevator dings, the doors open, and I hear Dad's frazzled voice. "My God, Clara!"

I look up quickly.

"*Shh*, Al," Mom says. She rushes over, crouches in front of me, and takes my hand. "Thank you, guys," she says to Sherry and Marisol.

"We didn't do a thing," Marisol says. "She was just keeping us company."

Mom pulls me toward her. "Honey—you cannot do that. You cannot run off like that. You absolutely may not ever—"

"I need to go to China," I say, standing up. Lola peeks out at me from behind Dad and gives me a thumbs-up. I ignore her. I feel like kicking her.

Mom stands up, too. All the nurses who had tried to help Lola are trying to look busy, but I can tell they are listening. Mom and Dad glance at each other. I don't want to be here, in this place where Lola died. I want to go to China, where she was born, so I say it again. "I have to go to China."

"Honey, it's just . . . it's expensive," Mom stammers. "And these kinds of things, they take planning, and—"

"There's a flight that leaves Wednesday night," I say.

"What?" Dad asks.

"There is."

"Sweetie, I'm sure it's exorbitant," he goes on. "And we can't just—"

"It's less than six hundred per person," I say quickly.

"You've researched it?" he asks, looking at Mom. "Six hundred?"

Sherry hands me a piece of tissue and I blow my nose. "I'm going." I know I sound like a brat; I *know* I can't go to China on my own. But I can't come up with anything else to say. "I'm going."

Mom and Dad look at each other for a minute, and then Mom puts her arm around my shoulder. "Let's go home," she says. "We can talk about everything there."

"Promise?" I ask.

"Promise."

Chapter 9

Yuming

I FALL ASLEEP with my cheek sticking to the bare mattress in the barracks, which, I have to admit, *is* better than the cement floor of the sewing room. I wake up the same way. The air is thick and hot, and next to me, Li, the smaller of the new boys, is still asleep, his thin chest rising and falling smoothly under a threadbare, stained sheet.

Older boys aren't allowed into the barracks where the young ones sleep, in case there's an inspection. Last night, Li refused to go without his brother. It reminded me of how close Bolin and I used to be when we were younger. Before he left.

Li had looked Mr. Zhang in the eye, little fists on tiny hips, and yelled, "No! I won't!"

His older brother, Kai, had wrapped his arm around his shoulder and nodded in approval, as if saying *I taught you well, little brother.* Mr. Zhang's eyes narrowed to slits in the almost-dark sewing room. I immediately thought of his tight grip on my arm outside of Molihua Park. I imagined Li crying quietly on a filthy mattress, surrounded by empty-eyed women, and I stepped forward. "I'll stay with him." I looked at Kai as I said it and saw relief on his face.

"You will owe me, then," Mr. Zhang said quickly. "Three extra hours of sewing. And if you speak with the women in the barracks . . ." He patted the pocket containing his knife.

I nodded.

Since arriving here, I'd avoided the barracks, mostly out of spite. I wasn't going to work overtime for Mr. Zhang for *anything*. This time, though, I'd thought, Weigh the options, picturing Kai's darting eyes.

Now, I turn over and study the ceiling in the morning light. It is low, cracked, and moldy, and I recall Kai's word yet again. It floats around my mind like Wai Po's lullaby.

Anywhere.

It's obvious what I need to do. I feel as though I'm outside my own body, as if I'm seeing myself as Wai Po and Wai Gong would see me. I'm too thin and dirty. I'm alone. I've lost everything and everyone, and I know what Wai Gong would advise.

Cloaked in the spirit of my old self, I look my new, *true* self over—from my raggedy pants, cinched at the waist with an old piece of discarded fabric, up to my bangs, which hang well below my eyes. *You'll be okay, Yuming,* I whisper into my own ear. *You've waited more than six weeks. Nothing is going to come of that note. It is clever and wise to come up with another plan.*

Next to me, Li stirs. I look down at his tiny body, wrapped in the thin, stained sheet, and I have an urge to wet my finger with spit and rub his cheeks clean. The paths of his tears—probably from days ago—are still visible on his filthy skin. I want to sing him one of Wai Po's songs.

He sighs deeply before slowly blinking his eyes open and taking in his surroundings. Then he bolts upright, reminding me of when I'd first arrived; how every morning I'd think before opening my eyes that maybe *this* was the day—the day I'd wake up in my old bed, with Wai Po and Wai Gong snoring soundly across the room. But even as I'd wished it, I'd known the truth. The cement floor pressing into my shoulder blades always told me the truth.

"Where's Kai?" Li asks immediately, rubbing his eyes.

I get up and fold his thin sheet. "In the sewing room," I whisper. His eyes fill with tears that threaten to make new rivers on his cheeks, and for a second, I look away. I lay the sheet on the mattress and reach for his hand. "I'll take you."

"Where's Mama?" he asks, standing up, disoriented.

"I don't know," I say softly.

He looks up at me, still bleary-eyed from sleep. "I need the toilet."

I nod and the woman on the mattress next to us points to the stairway across the hall. I'm not sure where we are in the factory, but I believe the stairs lead to the hallway behind the cafeteria.

At the bottom of the staircase, I open the bathroom door for Li and hold my breath as the foul odor rushes out. The walls of the tiny room are thin slats of wood that almost reach the ceiling, leaving a gap at the top so at least some fresh air can waft into the horrible-smelling enclosure. I peer through the cracks between the slats to see the barren side yard.

"I'll be right here," I tell Li, backing out. I feel exhausted despite having slept on the mattress. I turn on the faucet over the basin in the hallway and splash my face with icy water, thinking of the water pump behind our house. I wonder, again, if any of the neighbors are caring for our rice fields; the harvest is probably ready to be reaped now.

The bathroom door opens and Li steps into the hallway, where he rinses his hands. "Where's my brother?" he asks again.

"Come." I shake off the thoughts and memories and hold out my wet hand for his. "I'll take you."

I lead Li away from the cafeteria, down the windowless hallway, as Mr. Zhang told us we must do in the morning. We turn right at the end of the hall. Up ahead is the front entrance to the factory. Two men stand rigidly by the door. When they spot us, one of them walks briskly in our direction and guides us to the back of the factory, past the rows and rows of sewing women who don't look up, to the inconspicuous doorway that leads to the stairs down to our basement room.

I see Jing in the back, already hunched at her machine under a solitary row of lightbulbs. The rest of the lights are off, and the other children appear to be sleeping. I scour the floor, looking for Kai. Li is doing the same, and I suddenly feel panic. *We're not staying here,* I remember him saying. Would he have left his brother behind? I lead Li to our row, where, finally, he points to a figure on the floor in the far corner, just behind Jing. My heartbeat steadies.

Behind us come six quick taps at the door. I listen to it swing open but don't turn around. "Don't just sit there!" Mr. Zhang spits at the night guard. I hear the chair creak as the guard stands up and two clicks as Mr. Zhang locks the door. "Help me with the lights."

I smile at Jing before glancing over my shoulder to watch the guard and Mr. Zhang climb on benches to begin pulling the strings that hang from the overhead bulbs. Children rouse from sleep. A few get up and stand in line for the bathroom in the corner.

The adults have their backs to us. Li crouches and ruffles Kai's hair, and Kai sits up. I keep my eyes fixed on the two brothers as I pretend to focus on picking up fabric scraps from the floor under Jing. *We will leave soon,* Kai mouths silently to Li, and Li nods.

I look again to Mr. Zhang. He's busy yelling at two tiny girls as they wait in line for the toilet. The night guard walks atop the table two rows in front of us, pulling the lightbulbs on, one by one. I turn back to the boys.

"How will you get out?" I ask Kai quietly.

He stares at me, unblinking. "I don't know what you're talking about," he finally whispers.

I close my eyes. I see the black squares on the xiangqi boards at the park; I see the river separating the two sides of the boards; I see Wai Gong nodding at me and I open my eyes. "I know a way."

For a minute, Kai just squints at me, as if trying to make up his mind. I hear the night guard rustling on the tabletop behind us. Mr. Zhang is still screaming in the background. *Tell me,* Kai finally mouths.

I almost smile. I think one last time of the note—the note that, it appears, was a wasted risk—and I bend down to pick up a fabric scrap at Kai's feet.

"Okay," I whisper softly. "But if I do, I'm coming, too."

Chapter 10
July 2nd–3rd
Evanston, Illinois

Clara

AT HOME, MOM and Dad go into their bedroom to talk, and I lie in Lola's bed, the black hole swirling all around me. I try to fall asleep, because sometimes that makes the nothingness go away, but I can't.

I creep down the hall and press my ear to their closed door. "It's just that, ever since the funeral, I haven't been able to stop thinking that we made a mistake," Mom is saying in a low voice.

"I have no idea," Dad responds quietly. "I mean, it just didn't seem like she could handle being in there. I felt like, if she was saying she needed to be outside—"

"There's no question she's struggling," Mom interrupts. I hear her sniffling.

I feel like such a baby. I don't want to hear any more, and I tiptoe back to Lola's room and quietly shut her door.

Eventually, they go downstairs. I need to get this over with. If they're going to say no, it would be better to know now so I can come up with a new plan before that flight leaves on Wednesday. Because one way or another, I'm getting on that airplane.

In the kitchen, Mom and Dad are sitting at the table, flipping through some papers from a file folder. "Clara," Dad says, smiling at me gently, as if he's worried I'm going to break or something, "come sit on the couch with us."

He leads me over to the couch in the living room. Mom and I sit down, and I look at my knees. I can see the outline of Yuming's note and picture in my shorts pocket.

Dad glances quickly at Mom, and then walks over to the shelf where Lola's ashes are. My heart pounds as he picks up the carved wooden urn. "Clara," he starts, "when your sister was cremated . . ."

I don't want to see it—I don't want to see a container holding my sister's burnt body, and I turn my head away. But no matter where I look—out the window, at the floor, at the bookshelves—the image of a giant oven floats in front of me. I picture Lola being shoved inside. *I'm still alive!* she's screaming. The black hole slithers into the living room. It wraps itself around my throat and I tug at the neck of my T-shirt. I breathe in—*one, two, three*—and out—*one, two, three*.

Mom puts her arm around me. "Clara, sweetie, are you okay? You're all sweaty! Oh my God, lie back."

I should have been the one to die. Lola would have been strong enough to handle it. I put my head on Mom's lap.

She runs her fingers through my damp hair. The white ceiling looks sparkly and I wonder if I'm going crazy. "Al, I don't think—"

"Yeah," he says quietly, putting the urn back onto the shelf.

"You don't think what?" I ask weakly. "You don't think we can go to China?"

"No, it's not that at all," Dad says. "Just the opposite, actually."

I sit up. Blood rushes from my head back into my body.

"Here's the thing, Clara: Mom and I, well, we always thought that someday we'd all—the three of us—would make a trip back to China to . . ." He looks at the urn, then at Mom. "We always thought we'd make a trip back to China. We never really talked about when, exactly, but Mom and I are thinking that maybe we *should* go sooner than later."

He joins us on the couch. My heart is still beating way too fast, but the black hole isn't choking me anymore. "For your sake," Dad goes on. "For you. Maybe it will help you process Lola's death."

I close my eyes. I don't say anything.

"You did a good job researching flights," Mom adds. "You found an amazingly inexpensive one—especially for the summer. But it's to Beijing. We figured that when we went to China again, we would go to Shanghai—to visit Lola's park and the orphanage."

The ghost of my sister runs into the room, shaking her head— *Nooo!* she mouths to me. *Beijing! Yuming is outside of Beijing!*

"The flights to Shanghai are way more expensive, for some reason—" Mom continues, and I jump up.

"So let's fly to Beijing! We could do the same trip as last time. We could take the train to Shanghai after we see the Great Wall and Dan Temple, just like last time!"

"It's not a bad idea," Dad says slowly.

Lola is watching us, waiting, her face flushed.

Mom takes the laptop off the coffee table and opens it. It's already on the airline's website. "The flight to Beijing leaves in four days," Mom says skeptically, almost like she's talking to herself.

"The passports and visas are current, so we wouldn't have to go to the consulate," Dad reminds her.

"But there's work. . . ." Mom goes on. "How on *earth* would we—"

"Well, let's make some calls," Dad interrupts. All of a sudden, he sounds like a little kid, and I look from his eager face to Mom's. She's biting her lower lip. "You call Caryn," Dad urges. "I'll call Russ. He'd said that he wanted to sub as much as he could this summer."

Mom nods. "Can we afford this?" she asks Dad. "I mean, I know the answer. Of course we can't. . . ." It looks like she's trying not to smile now.

"Definitely not," Dad says, but he's smiling, too.

"Okay," Mom finally says, kissing my cheek. "Okay. We'll make the calls." She points her finger at me. "Don't get too excited yet."

The rest of the day crawls by. I jump every time the phone rings. By dinnertime Caryn has agreed to cover for Mom at work, and when I wake up the next morning, Dad is standing over me, grinning like a little boy. "Russ said yes!"

"Are you serious?" I ask, bolting upright in bed.

He hugs me. "Mom is calling the doctor to see if we need any immunizations."

"I can't believe it!"

Dad looks me in the eye. "Mom and I think this is important," he says, not blinking. "We think this is something that you *need*."

You have no idea, I want to scream, but I don't—I don't say anything. I try not to smile.

"Okay, then," Dad says. "China, here we come!"

Yuming, here I come!

Chapter 11
July 3rd–6th
Hebei Province, China

Yuming

MY MIND RACES in the dreary sewing room as Li and I stand over Kai. I recall the shimmering image of my former self that visited me in the barracks this morning, and I know with certainty that I can no longer wait around for somebody to rescue me. It's time for me to rescue myself. I smile as I think of this; Wai Gong would be proud.

Behind us, Mr. Zhang has finished screaming at the two girls in line. They stand side by side, as if frozen. "Go to the toilet and then get to work!" he shouts crazily at nobody in particular before heading back to the door, unlocking it, and slipping out. Four thin boys—whose backs I have been staring at for months—make their way to their seats in the row ahead of us just as the night guard hops off their table and heads for his chair, checking his watch. Any minute now, the next guard will take his place.

"Fine," Kai whispers angrily. "What's your great idea, then?" His voice is harsh and bitter. Slowly, deliberately, he bends down to fold the large scrap of fabric he was lying on so the guard doesn't see him talking. The chugging of sewing machines grows louder around us.

"Get to your machines!" the guard yells across the room. "What's taking so long in the back corner?"

My heart jumps. I look from Kai to Li, then over Jing's head to the guard. *Jing.* I feel a pang of guilt for not including her, but surely the more people involved, the riskier the plan becomes. The door swings open behind the night guard again and the day guard enters. The night guard turns his back for a moment. Swiftly, I whisper my idea to Kai.

☆

At lunch later that week, Kai, Li, and I gulp down our food even more quickly than usual. After days of waiting, Mrs. Ma, the least-cruel-seeming cook, and Mr. Sun, the guard with the voice that is the least sharp, are finally on duty at the same time. I watch Kai take a deep breath before giving Li a quick shove. Li slides off the bench, curls his tiny body into a ball, and begins to wail and moan. It's so realistic that for a moment I worry that he *is,* coincidentally, having actual stomach pains.

Li rocks back and forth, shrieks once, and is quiet. I jump out of my seat and kneel beside him on the floor as Jing and a few of the others stand to watch us. I stroke his hair. "Li? Are you all right?"

Mrs. Ma walks toward us. Li winks up at Kai and me before he wails again, turns onto his hands and knees, and rests his cheek on the filthy ground.

"My brother!" Kai leaps to his feet when Mrs. Ma arrives at our side. "He is ill!"

"What's happening?" she asks. Mr. Sun joins us.

"My brother is ill!" Kai says again. I watch in shock as tears jump from his eyes, and I look away, down at Li's dirty hair.

"I'm going to be sick," Li moans.

"Not in here, you're not," Mr. Sun responds quickly.

"I can't help it!" Li curls into a ball again. "My stomach."

"So get to the courtyard," he snaps, pushing at Li with his foot.

"I need the bathroom," Li whispers.

"Come, Li," I say, pulling him gently. "Come on."

Li stands, wobbly, still hunched at the waist. "I can't walk. I need my brother."

Kai takes his other arm.

"The three of you are not permitted to leave the cafeteria," Mr. Sun says, as if he's reciting a rule from a sheet of paper.

I look across to Kai, panicked. *Now what?* This wasn't part of our plan. Li expertly falls to the ground, moaning again. "I can't stand. I'm going to be sick. I need the toilet."

I shrug and force myself not to smile at his acting skill. "We'll each have to take an arm," I say. Li begins to cough. "Unless one of you will help him?" I look from Mrs. Ma to Mr. Sun. Li gags.

"Just go," Mrs. Ma says quickly, Mr. Sun nodding in agreement. I look down so she won't see my dishonest eyes. Kai and I take hold of Li, and we hobble together toward the door at the back of the cafeteria. If our plan succeeds, I'll never see this room again. I quicken my pace.

I open the door with my free hand and, my heart thudding with nervousness and excitement, we push our way through. I don't look back. When Kai pulls the door shut behind us, the three of us glance at one another for a moment. No adults in sight. Already I feel free. *Do not be foolish, Yuming,* Wai Gong would say, though. *Do not be careless.*

I peer into the dim, empty hallway with the stairway to the barracks on the second floor. Across from the stairs is the bathroom.

"Hurry," Kai demands, and we run toward the bathroom— the one I took Li to less than a week ago. It feels like that was a different lifetime. For a minute, just a minute, I think of Bo's knotted pink scar and wonder what the consequence would be if Mr. Zhang were to discover us bolting down the hall, Li not ill after all. But I force myself to stop. *Concentrate, Yuming,* Wai Po and Wai Gong would tell me whenever they could see that my mind was wandering from my studies. *Concentrate.*

I motion to the bathroom. When we arrive at the doorway, it is open, as if waiting for us. Suddenly, I think I hear footsteps behind us. I spin around, but the hallway is empty, the door to the cafeteria still shut. Kai grabs my hand, pulls Li and me into the bathroom, and silently closes the door.

The foul smell envelops us. I breathe through my mouth, but the odor is so thick that it weaves its way into my nose anyway. The room is tiny. Outside light shines in through the gaps between the slats and the opening near the roof. The three of us crowd by the door to avoid the filthy rectangular hole in the cracked clay floor.

Flies buzz, dive in and out of the opening in the ground, and swarm around our faces. A wave of nausea rises in me, but Kai and Li seem unfazed.

"So, what's the next part of your plan?" Kai whispers, suddenly sarcastic, as he eyes the opening above that is too high to reach.

My response is prevented by a quick, quiet knocking at the door.

I freeze.

Kai, Li and I look to one another. Li clears his throat. "Occupied!" he calls out innocently, and I breathe a sigh of relief for this tiny con artist who, at probably seven years old, may possess more wisdom than I do.

There's another knock, more urgent this time.

"I said I'm busy!"

Kai nods at Li approvingly.

"Hurry!" a familiar voice whispers from outside the door. "Mr. Sun just left the cafeteria to find Mr. Zhang and tell him one of the new boys is ill."

I glance from Kai to Li again, reach for the door handle, and swing it open. Jing slides inside.

She scrunches her nose at the smell and shudders. "I'm coming with you."

I stare at her face—at her expression of quiet determination. She must have heard us planning, days ago, in the sewing room. I watch, speechless, as she pulls a pair of the sharpest sewing scissors out of a thin knapsack that's hidden beneath her too-large white T-shirt. My stomach twists. Jing has always been kind and quick to offer sewing help, and now—now she stands crowded against us with a scissors in her hand.

"What do you think—" Kai begins.

"How did you get out of the cafeteria?" I interrupt.

She gives us a sly smile. "It must be contagious, what Li has," she says. "Once Mr. Sun left the cafeteria, Mrs. Ma certainly didn't want to deal with another sick prisoner by herself."

I am overcome with remorse. All the nights Jing and I had slept side by side on the sewing room floor, all the whispered snippets of conversation we had exchanged when nobody could hear, all the times she had passed me the seam ripper before I even had to ask for it . . . While Kai, Li, and I had been planning our escape this past week, Jing had obviously been planning hers, too. I should have included her from the beginning.

"Once Mr. Sun finds Mr. Zhang, we'll have very little time," she says, urging me back to the present. "There aren't many places Mr. Zhang could be, and there aren't many bathrooms we could be in, so turn around," she says to me, ignoring Kai's harsh glare.

"Jing?" I ask.

"We need to be smart about this," she goes on. "Who do you think Mr. Zhang will tell the police to look for? Two girls and two raggedy-looking boys. So, turn around, Yuming."

I'm frozen.

"All right, then," she says, nodding. "Me first." My pulse races. She points the scissors toward her delicate face and cuts off a large handful of long hair.

I take a deep breath as she tosses the dark strands into the filthy hole in the ground. "Some help in back?" she asks. I nod and take the scissors, grateful for her presence and brimming with shame for excluding her. I try to clear my mind. *Think rationally,* Wai Gong would say.

I attempt to focus on her black hair as I cut it quickly, but my mind wanders to Wai Po and the wooden stool she would pull in front of our mirror whenever my bangs began to tickle my eyelashes. She'd stand over me, the wrinkles on her face soft and deep, steady her shaking hands, and trim my bangs in a neat line. Then I'd sweep the black cuttings out the doorway. They'd blow over the fields. *Now you're everywhere*, Wai Po told me once, coming up behind me as I watched the tufts disappear over the rice crop.

I cut the back of Jing's hair in a straight line, from the bottom of one ear to the other. Kai kicks stray hairs into the deep hole in the floor as I work. When Jing turns around, I look down.

"Jing—" I start.

"It's okay," she says.

"But I should have—"

"Who is next?" she interrupts. "We need to hurry."

"I'll make it up to you," I tell her suddenly without thinking, handing her the scissors. I don't know what makes me say it, but she smiles, as if accepting my apology.

"Quick, turn around," she demands, so I do.

When she's done with the two boys and me, we scrunch together and peer into the smudged mirror tacked to the back of the door. Our white T-shirts, produced in the front of the factory, are identical; our haircuts—identical. My heart thumps. We need to move quickly.

"Now," Jing says, "how will we get over?"

"Jing is the tallest," Kai, who has been quiet since her arrival, says. "She should go last."

I look at him. "How will she get over with nobody to help her?"

"She'll have to jump," he replies curtly.

I glance around. There's not a thing in the bathroom to stand on. It's just the four of us, the human waste deep down in the hole, now covered with our hair, and the flies. I catch a glimpse of my face again in the dirty mirror. I don't even recognize myself—the once-happy girl, number one in her class, from Yemo Village.

The mirror.

I pull it away from the door. It snaps off easily, with nothing but dry, yellowed glue coating its back. Jing and Li move to the side as Kai and I lean it against the wall. It's higher than our knees, but thin. "Do you think you can do it?" I ask Jing.

She studies the mirror and doesn't reply.

"I can do it," Kai finally says, sighing.

"He's an expert climber," Li chimes in. Somehow I don't doubt it, and I wonder where these two boys came from.

"All right, then," I say to Kai and Jing. "Me first, because I'm the shortest of the three of us. I'll need the biggest push to get over. Then Li. I can help him over from the other side. Then Jing, and then Kai." It feels as if we've been in the bathroom forever. Mr. Sun could easily have located Mr. Zhang by now. At any time he could arrive outside the thin door. "We need to hurry."

Li looks to his brother, who nods in approval of my plan, and I jump for the opening as Kai and Jing push me up by the backside. In a second, I'm grasping the splintery wood at the top of the wall and feeling air on my face, blowing the scent of the toilet away. The side yard is empty aside from a few lonely bushes scattered atop the packed dirt. Off in the distance, to one direction, is the forest that leads to the rolling foothills of the mountains. In the other direction, beyond the front of the factory, a hill slopes downward into a bright-green valley. At the bottom of the valley is a village. I look back to the forest. Seeing the tightly packed trees, probably less than half a kilometer away, sends an explosion of excitement, energy, and fear through me. I throw my right leg over the wall, duck under the tin roof, and let myself over to the other side.

It takes a bit longer to get Li in position, because he's so small. As I listen to Kai and Jing struggle, I check over my shoulder constantly. How long until Mr. Zhang comes after us? Finally, I see through the slats that Kai has Li on his shoulders. Soon, Li's small hands appear overhead. He scrambles over, and I catch his light body.

With a quiet rustling, Jing effortlessly lowers herself onto our side, her knapsack flopping against her back. Now for Kai. We probably left the cafeteria more than fifteen minutes ago. How long it will take him to get over on his own? For a second, the fear overcomes me and I even contemplate running for the woods—the nearest place to hide—but I can't, especially after already excluding Jing. "Hurry, Kai!" I whisper.

Through the slats, I see Kai's feet trying to balance on the top of the thin, fragile mirror. In the distance, I hear men's voices. My heart begins to knock against the inside of my chest. I think the voices are coming from inside the factory, but with the sound of my ragged breath and the thumping pulse in my ears, I can't be certain. I twirl around again to make sure there is nobody outside coming for us. With panic on their faces, Jing and Li do the same.

"Someone is coming!" Jing whispers. "The voices are coming from inside!"

"Go without me," Kai demands. "There are at least two people coming down the hall right now!"

"No," Li replies before I can even take a breath. I look to the woods and back down at him. There are tears in his eyes and his hands are balled into fists.

"Li." Kai's voice is firm as he struggles to balance on the top of the mirror. "Run now. Hide nearby. I'll meet up with you. I promise."

I reach for Li's hand, but he yanks it away from me. "No," he repeats. I look again to the woods that are so close, and then back to Jing. She glances nervously toward the front of the factory. Through the slats in the wall, Kai's feet struggle to find balance on a piece of glass that's surely about to break below him. I picture myself in our mirror back home again, my hair damp and even, Wai Po behind me, smiling over my shoulder.

The voices come again from inside, through the thin bathroom door. They're louder now, but I can't make out what they're saying. "Come, Kai, hurry!" I whisper.

"Run! I'll find you!"

"No!" Li's voice again—small, but hard. "I'm staying here."

"Take him!" Kai insists.

"Jump, Kai!" Jing pleads. We both know Li won't go anywhere without his brother. I see one foot on the top of the mirror, the other on the ground, and the leap. The mirror shatters into a pile of glass as Kai's hands appear above our heads. His feet shuffle against the wall, and he grunts with effort.

Mr. Zhang's voice comes to us from the hallway on the other side of the flimsy wooden door. It's angry and quick. "Has anyone checked this one?"

"I'm not sure, sir," another voice answers from farther away.

Kai's leg appears overhead and Jing and I reach for it. A trickle of blood seeps from under his trousers; a shard must have cut him. He lands with a quiet moan and grabs Li's hand. "Run!" he whispers to the three of us, pointing to the woods, but we are already running.

"Who is in here? Who. Is. In. Here?" Mr. Zhang's voice demands through the door, through the foul-smelling enclosure, through the rotting wooden slats, through the open summer air, along airwaves that vibrate through smog and mountain wind—wind that picks up dust from the yard and carries it into the valley below, wind that whistles past my ears as Jing, Kai, Li, and I sprint away from the pale-pink factory.

Jing peers over her shoulder as we barrel toward the woods. "Nobody behind us yet!" she pants, and then the only sounds are our pounding feet and quick breathing. We're halfway there, halfway to safety.

My legs move automatically. They feel loose, as though connected to my body only by threads. I remember physical education classes at school—the fifty-meter dash, the one-hundred-meter run, awards for the fastest runners—and I could laugh now at how juvenile it all seems. I want to look behind us, but I cannot will my head to turn. I keep my gaze fixed on the woods at the bottom of the mountains that loom, brown, jagged, and tree covered, before us.

Somehow, Li keeps up with us, his tiny legs pumping almost effortlessly.

"The bathroom door was locked, but only with a small hook," Kai says, panting, as our quick footsteps stir up a cloud of dust that I wish could magically transport me home, to my old life—to Wai Po and Wai Gong. To Bolin. "Anyone who wants to bust through that door will be able to do so in no time."

I review the timeline as we dodge bushes and shrubs. Mr. Zhang would have called out a few times, demanding to know who was in the bathroom. When nobody answered, he would have tried the door and found it locked. He would have called out again, threateningly, and then burst through. He would have seen the broken mirror. He would have figured it out; he would have figured *everything* out.

We are almost to the woods. Fifty meters to go. The humid air presses down like it's trying to drown me, but I will not let it. Wai Gong, I think, I am doing it.

Mr. Zhang would have raced down the hallway and turned right at the end, the guard close behind him. He would have pushed the two men stationed at the front door to the side.

I run on legs unused to exercise, breathing in dust and smog.

The two men would have stumbled, surprised, and asked what was happening. Mr. Zhang and the guard would have exploded through the doors into the thick, smoggy air, twirling around, hunting for us like animals.

The packed dirt is turning to grass beneath my feet. I am breathing quickly through my nose, my jaw clenched.

Mr. Zhang and his guard would have two choices: to run toward the road to the village or to run toward the mountains. Perhaps one would have gone one way, and one the other.

A tree branch slaps my cheek and I shut my eyes instinctively.

Everything depends on this—on *their* decision—on *their* guess as to where we went.

High grasses at the edge of the woods whip my thighs.

What would they decide?

We dive into the grass.

The quiet sounds of nature are thick around us, like a blanket. The chirping of crickets combines with the sounds of our breathing. A leaf sticks to my nose as I inhale, flutters against flattened grass as I exhale. Jing's face is next to mine, her trimmed bangs clumpy with sweat, and I lock my eyes on her. *I am sorry,* I want to tell her. I am overcome with fear; I am overcome with guilt.

"Forgive me," I say and she nods quickly, as if she understands, as if she understands everything: why I excluded her, where I came from, and where I need to go, even though I know that she cannot know all of that.

"We need to move," she whispers, her hands already positioned by her side to push herself up. "Mr. Zhang could easily assume that we ran here. Unless they think that we headed to the village, they'll be in the woods in no time."

I nod and lift my head slightly. The grass around us is probably two feet tall, but Jing is right—we are not safe yet. Several meters ahead, the trees thicken and rise as the foothills slope up toward the mountains.

I am millions of worlds away from home.

Hidden, I hope, by the grass, we crawl like soldiers toward the tree line. I allow myself to peer cautiously back toward the factory. The side yard is empty—either because Mr. Zhang and his men assumed we went the other way, or because they're already in the grasses or the woods, waiting for us to appear so they can drag us back and punish us like Bo was punished. Or worse.

We reach the area where the woods thicken and stand cautiously. I have never been in a forest like this, and I wonder what kind of dangers might lurk in it. When we see no sign of any pursuers, we bolt again, leaping over dead branches and darting between ancient trees. At last, we are no longer able to make out the factory behind us. Ahead of us, the ground is rocky, and mountain bluffs loom.

We pick our way toward a wall of rock with an indentation like a shallow cave. Without speaking, we inch our way into it, feetfirst and on our bellies, until the overhang covers our bodies. Only our heads protrude.

"There could be snakes in here," I whisper.

"Could be . . ." Jing says, panting, resting her cheek on the thin knapsack.

"I'd take snakes over Mr. Zhang any day," Kai says, his face glinting with sweat.

"Yeah," Li agrees. "I like snakes, anyway." He yawns. "You were born in the year of the snake, Kai-Kai. Can we sleep now?"

"Yes, we'll sleep now," Kai says. "When the sun starts to set, we'll head for the village."

Chapter 12

Clara

UPSTAIRS IN MY room, I open the family laptop and study the map of Hebei Province for the millionth time. I look from Beijing, in the center of the province, to the thick, jagged mountains to the north. My red suitcase is already packed and waiting in the middle of my room, even though we aren't leaving until the day after tomorrow. Downstairs, Dad just got off the phone with his brother in Spain and now he's on the phone with Grandma. I imagine her sitting in her kitchen in Minneapolis, picking nervously at her nail polish. *Are you sure this is a good idea, Al?* she's probably asking. *Are you sure you and Elise can afford it? With all those hospital bills?* I want to shake Lola in excitement. *We're really doing this!* I scream to her in my mind before looking back to the screen.

Yuming wrote that she was a few hours outside of Beijing, in Hebei Province, but who knows where, exactly? I mean, Hebei Province is probably the same size as *Illinois*. I ignore this thought because it makes me feel kind of sick, and I open up a Beijing city map. I trace the outline of the massive city with my eyes—the miles and miles of land—before closing the Internet window. I wonder what Yuming is doing now. Almost two months have passed since she wrote the note.

The summer that I was going into first grade, we went to Minneapolis for a month. I barely remember anything about the trip, but I do remember that Lola had a huge argument with Mom and Dad before we left. I was standing in her doorway, confused, watching her scream and stomp her feet. Her blue suitcase was on her bed, crammed full with all her stuffed animals.

Where are we going to put your clothes? Mom had asked, baffled, as she stood next to Lola's bed. I could tell she was trying not to smile, and I ran to Lola's side.

Don't laugh! I had demanded.

Dad came in, a stack of folded laundry in his arms. *What's going on in here?* He looked Lola, her suitcase, and me over, and then raised his eyebrows at Mom.

Now you're laughing at me, too! Lola had screamed, her hands on her hips, tears flying out of her eyes. *It's not funny!*

I remember studying her, confused. How *was* she going to bring any clothes? And why *would* she want all of her stuffed animals to come with us? We were just going to Grandma Betty's. I dug through her suitcases. There were animals in there that I didn't even know she had. They must have been buried under her bed for years.

I turned to Mom and Dad and put my hands on my hips, just like Lola. *This is Lola's suitcase,* I said. *She can pack whatever she wants.*

The room was silent, except for the sounds of Lola sniffling.

Honey, Mom had finally said, crouching in front of Lola, her face serious, *are you worried about what's going to happen to your animals when you're gone?*

I cannot leave anyone *behind,* Lola had declared. *Not one animal. How do you think it would feel to be completely left behind?* Tears were streaming down her face.

Mom had nodded and wiped her own eyes, and Dad had gone to the phone that used to be on the table in the hallway. It was tan with black buttons. I wonder where it went—I haven't thought of that phone in forever.

He called Valerie, who lived across the street and sometimes babysat for us. After he talked to her for a few minutes, we piled all of Lola's stuffed animals, except for one small green alligator, into our plastic wagon and pulled it across the street. Valerie told Lola that she'd look after them, free of charge, until we got home, and she never smiled, not even a little bit.

Valerie lives in New York now. I haven't seen her since the funeral.

I look at the date on my phone, as if staring at it will make July sixth come sooner. I open the weather app and check the forecast for Beijing. It's hot and humid with rain likely in the evenings—the same as the last time we were there. *Hang tight, Yuming,* I say in my head. *I'm on my way.*

☆

By Wednesday, I'm starting to feel like I might be going completely crazy. Every time I look at the clock, I add fourteen hours to the time and try to imagine what Yuming might be doing. Is she working? Eating? I wonder where she sleeps. I remember the mountains that we could see from our hotel window in Beijing, and I picture Yuming sitting at a sewing machine, looking out a window at those very same mountains.

I find the laptop in Mom and Dad's room and send the two maps that I saved to the printer. As I do, a wave of panic washes over me. We're leaving in a few hours and I still haven't figured out how I'm going to convince Mom and Dad that we should find and visit a factory prison that's a few hours outside of the city.

Eh, you'll figure it out, Lola would say. *You've got a long flight ahead of you—to think.* I can practically see her grinning at me over the banister as I walk downstairs to collect my maps.

Mom is standing next to the sink, rummaging through a cabinet. "Hey, honey, did you print something out, or was that Dad?" She puts a bottle of Advil into a Ziploc of toiletries.

"It was me," I say calmly. The second map is pulsing its way out of the printer. Mom zips up the plastic bag and walks past me, toward the stairs.

"Oh, maps?" she asks, glancing over my shoulder.

"Yeah, I thought it would be cool to know ahead of time what's what."

Mom stops and smiles at me. She has dark circles under her eyes. "I guess last time we were in China you were just a kid, huh?"

"I guess so." I'm sure Mom is thinking about the fact that I'm growing up and Lola isn't, and I can't bear the thought of that. "So we're leaving in an hour?"

She looks at her watch. "An hour and a half."

I nod and run up the stairs with my maps, past the smiling ghost of my sister.

In my bedroom, I fold the papers and tuck them into the inside pocket of my pink backpack next to the copies of Yuming's note and photograph. I have to come up with a plan, and time is running out.

Help me, Lola, I think. I need to find the pink factory that's *somewhere* outside the capital of China. I need to somehow get us there. And then, I need to figure out how to get Yuming out.

Chapter 13
Hebei Province, China
July 6th

Yuming

WHEN I WAKE up, the sky is dark gray. Wind wildly rustles the leaves, branches snap and sway, and fear washes over me. I can't believe I took the risk of sleeping. What would Wai Gong think?

Groggily, I inch my way out from the tiny cave and massage the back of my head, which is sore from the rutted stone that I *somehow* allowed myself to fall asleep on. Still tucked under the overhang of rock, Kai twitches in his sleep. On top of the ledge, Li sits in Jing's lap as she sings him a soft song. Like Wai Po used to do with me.

I rub my eyes and try to clear my head. "What time do you think it is?" I feel disoriented. Could it be dawn? Could Mr. Zhang and his men be watching us right now, waiting for the perfect opportunity to leap out, grab us, and drag us back to the factory?

"I'd guess it's probably just after dinnertime," Jing says. Li is playing with her long fingers.

I nod. Dinnertime. "I'm hungry."

Li looks up from Jing's hands. "Me, too," he says quickly, checking around Jing's back as if a meal might magically appear from behind her.

"I don't think it's safe to stay here much longer," I say to Jing. "We should get as far away from the factory as we can."

She nods, gently pushes Li off her lap, and stands and squints into the woods that shielded us when we escaped. "Well," she says, "it's getting dark. That's good."

"We should get through the woods before nightfall," Kai mumbles. I turn to him. His eyes are still closed.

"That's true," I say, moving toward the trees. "We should go."

Kai pulls himself out of the crevice and stretches. "That bed makes the sewing room benches seem luxurious," he says.

The wind picks up and dark clouds tumble in the gray sky. I don't know how Kai can joke at a time like this. Now that I'm out of the factory, I'm more eager than ever to get to a train or a bus—anything that will take me south. I can just picture it: The door will close behind me, I'll wave to Jing and the boys, and I'll be off—back to Shanghai, and then home to Yemo Village.

But how can I board a bus or a train without money?

An owl screams in the woods, and I look around again. The mountain range towers behind us, mushroom colored in the dusk. Before us is the narrow stretch of forest. As Li and Jing hop down off the rocky ledge and join me, the question bullies its way into my mind again: How, in this country of a billion and a half people, will I ever find my brother? I swallow hard. Behind the question slithers the phrase *this life is not my life*; *this life is not my life*, but I silence it, because, for now, this life *is* my life.

"Come on," Kai urges, heading into the woods. I try to shut off my thoughts as I follow him.

In the dying light we stumble over dead branches, under low-hanging boughs, and around gnarled trunks as we head in the direction of the village. Maybe we could find food there, and a place to hide for the night. We all are aware—too aware—that to get to the village, we will need to pass the factory.

I can imagine Mr. Zhang yelling at one of his paid police officers this very moment, furiously pounding his fist on a desk as he describes us, knowing that if his secret leaks outside his inner circle, he'll surely go to prison. That idea makes me smile, despite my aching legs, empty stomach, and parched throat.

Daylight is completely gone now; the hazy moon appears and disappears as clouds blow across the sky. It smells like rain.

Kai taps my arm and motions to our left. Jing and I nod. The air is thick with humidity, and light from the moon occasionally filters into the forest. I can't help but think of Wai Po sitting on the edge of my bed, singing, *The moon is bright, the wind is quiet, tree leaves hang over your window . . .*

Her song runs through my mind over and over as we weave our way through the woods. As though in a trance, I barely feel the branches that scrape at my arms. When we near the edge of the forest, we stop, panting, and peer out into the darkness, searching for the factory.

Jing points. It's to our right, a little way behind us now—a dark, angular mass against the night sky. Soot from its smokestacks is just barely illuminated by the dim light that seeps from the windows. In the basement of the factory, completely hidden from view, twenty children are surely sewing in the hidden room.

But I can't think of them—not now. First I need to save myself; that's what Wai Gong would tell me. I'm relieved to see that we've traveled farther than I thought. A narrow dirt road leads down to the valley below, where lights from the small village twinkle in the black night.

"That will be the road into town," Kai whispers, pointing. "Let's take it."

I look at Jing. "I don't think so," she says quickly, and I nod, relieved that she and I are in agreement.

"Definitely not," I add. "Too risky. If Mr. Zhang isn't in the woods, he could be on the road. Better to walk down the hill here."

Kai seems surprised to be challenged, but he shrugs and we begin to make our way down, through tall grass and prickly bushes. It doesn't feel as steep as it appeared from above, but when the moon peeks out, I can see that the hill flattens to our right, next to the road. Kai seems to have noticed the same thing.

"Let's at least walk in that direction a bit," he says, pointing. "We don't have to take the road."

We head downward and toward the right, the tiny village growing slightly brighter as we descend. *Think, Yuming,* Wai Gong would say. *How will you do this? Once you arrive in the village, you'll need to stay hidden and get money. That will be tricky.*

A challenge, Wai Gong, I think. *You know I like a challenge.*

"Get down!" Jing suddenly whispers. I look around for a second before Kai grabs my arm with one hand and Li's with the other. The four of us fall to our knees in the tall grass. "Lower," Kai whispers. I plaster myself to the earth. A car is rumbling behind us and to our right. We are much closer to the road than I'd realized.

My heart pounds. Crickets screech. The car is traveling slowly—perhaps because the road is bad, or perhaps because the driver is searching for four runaways. My pulse thuds against the earth into which I wish I could somehow burrow and disappear. The headlights paint the grass a dark, shimmering green. I want to close my eyes, but I don't let myself. *Let us be hidden,* I pray. *Wai Po, Wai Gong, let us be hidden.*

"It could be anyone," I whisper, as much to calm myself as the others. Next to me, Li whimpers a little, and Kai puts his finger to his lips. I grab Jing's hand and we all watch, our bellies flat on the hillside, as the car creeps by, no more than fifteen meters from us. The windows are down and exhaust rolls over us. The car is parallel to us now; it is so, so close.

Through the grass I can make out Mr. Zhang's wife in the driver's seat, her hair pulled into a tight bun, her scowl illuminated by the moonlight. In the passenger seat is a man, his head fully out the window, searching the other side of the road with a flashlight. It could be one of the guards or Mr. Zhang himself. I can't tell.

I want to look and I don't want to look. For some reason, I recall Wai Gong's dead body, still and cold in his bed, and how I'd wanted to both run from it and stay with it. I squeeze my eyes closed, like I did that morning I found him. I'd made a wish that he would be alive when I opened them again. But it didn't work; he was gone. He is a spirit now, I had thought, tears streaming down my cheeks.

I open my eyes. The car is crawling even more slowly than it was a moment ago—so slowly that it has nearly stopped. It has just passed us, and the man's head is still sticking out of the passenger window, his flashlight painting flickering green lines on the grass across the road. Mrs. Zhang is staring straight ahead. The car bumps over a pothole and she curses.

"Ouch!" the man cries—it's the night guard. "My head! Are you not looking?" I hear him bark. "What good are you if you cannot both drive *and* look at the same time?" I wonder where Mr. Zhang is.

Mrs. Zhang turns her head to her left, toward us, and her rodent-like face scours the hillside. She rolls her eyes. Jing squeezes my hand. I hold my breath.

The car bumps over another rut and Mrs. Zhang looks straight ahead, cursing again. She maneuvers the car around it before poking her head out the window one more time. To spot us now, she or the guard would have to get out and look behind the car, or turn it around on the narrow, one-lane road. But they continue to creep forward. I breathe a sigh of relief and roll onto my back.

I look up at the patches of faint stars between the clouds. Though I am probably more than a thousand kilometers from home, they are the same stars that Wai Gong and I sometimes gazed at when we sat at the edge of the rice field in the months after Wai Po died.

"Thank you, Wai Gong," I whisper.

"From us, too," Kai adds, and I giggle. Only the orange rear lights of Mrs. Zhang's car are visible now, and Jing begins to giggle, too. Soon the four of us are laughing so hard it feels like there's a knife in my side, but I don't mind it.

"I need to tell you something, Kai-Kai," Li says, hysterical.

Kai smacks him on the head. "Don't call me that. What?"

"I am going to pee."

We all burst into more laughter. Kai sits up, wiping tears from his eyes. "So go in the grass. You'll have to go pants-less if you ruin your only pair."

Li pops up and runs several feet away before we hear what sounds like water rushing from the pump back home, and the three of us burst into laughter again. "Stop laughing," Li whispers. "I can't pee and laugh at the same time."

He returns to us and, with my stomach sore from laughter, I scour the dark stretch of road. Mrs. Zhang's car is nowhere to be seen. "They'll get to town, search for us, and then drive back up here," I whisper. "Hopefully, we'll arrive after they have left."

"Yup," Kai agrees.

We walk farther from the road and slowly make our way toward the twinkling lights of the village. My shoes and pants are soaked with dew, and the scrapes on my hands and knees sting, but I don't care. Bolin, I will find you, I think. Somehow. . . .

☆

The village is even smaller than it appeared from higher up. We silently cross a farmer's field, picking our way carefully through rows of wheat, and creep by a small home where perhaps a family is asleep. I have no idea what time it is. Across a dirt road is a small row of closed stores, a few of them shuttered with metal doors, as protection from thieves. We stand in an alley at the end of the street, considering our options. We have to eat soon—my stomach feels hollow.

Kai wipes the sweat from his face with his shirt, exposing his bony torso, before putting his hands on his hips, obviously thinking. Li moves from Jing's side to stand next to his brother. He puts his hands on his hips, mimicking Kai. I can't believe how far he has walked without complaining.

We start walking toward the stores. When we get close, I hear men's voices talking and laughing in the distance. Perhaps there's a bar on the next street. "Let's go talk to them," Kai says, jerking his head in the direction of the sounds.

"No!" I say immediately. "Mr. Zhang has probably told them to be on the lookout for four runaways!"

"No way," Kai replies quickly. "Then they'd know he has children working for him. He'd never tell. And anyway, I don't believe that he works with the police; he was just trying to scare us."

Li nods. "You should trust my brother," he says solemnly.

"How trustworthy could he be if you two ended up in the factory?" Jing asks Li, smiling a little.

Li looks at Kai, surprised, and then shrugs. "I'm going to see what's over that way, Kai-Kai." He points to the end of the row of stores and wanders off.

For a moment, Kai, Jing, and I look at one another. I feel strangely nervous, waiting to hear Jing's response to Kai's latest suggestion. "It's not worth the risk," she finally says, and I quietly breathe a sigh of relief.

Kai shrugs like Li did.

"Hey, Kai, come have a look!" Li calls from the corner.

Kai trots off, but I am too hungry to expend any extra energy. I sit down, my back against a bumpy corrugated metal door, and empty the dirt and pebbles from my wet shoes. Jing does the same. My feet are covered with blisters. It's strange not to feel hair in my face as I lean over and try to examine my heels. I know I should not let my guard down yet—the Zhangs are just up the hill, barely out of sight—but my heartbeat is starting to settle, like a row of sewing machines slowing down.

"Look at this blister," Jing says, holding up her foot. She's smiling, like she's proud of it.

"Jing," I ask her, "how long were you in the factory?"

"Four years and eleven months," she answers without hesitation.

I swallow hard. "Almost five years?"

She nods.

"And how old are you?"

"Thirteen."

"Me, too. So you were there since you were—"

"Probably just a bit older than Li," she answers quickly. She's pressing at her blister with her thumb.

"How did you end up there, anyway?" I ask her.

"My family needed money." She says it matter-of-factly, offering no hint of her feelings about it.

I nod. I don't know how else to respond. "Well, after five years in the factory, no wonder you look so happy to have a nasty blister," I finally say.

"You know, Yuming, if it weren't for you, I'd still—"

I look away, remorseful once again, and I'm relieved when Kai's voice interrupts her.

"Yuming! Jing! Come here!"

Jing leaps up, wiggles her foot back into her wet shoe, and reaches down to me, as if forgiving me for my selfishness. "Thank you," she says, and I nod, even though I didn't do anything—I did less than nothing. Besides, if Kai and Li hadn't arrived, I'd still be there, too.

I let Jing pull me up and we half run, half limp down the block to where Kai is standing. All the way there, I watch Jing gawk at the unfamiliar surroundings. *Five years.* I remember Bolin telling me about war prisoners who, once released, went crazy because they no longer knew how to operate as a part of society. As I study her face, she turns and smiles at me. I think of the sharp scissors—the ones with the orange handle—and how she knew her way around the factory. I think of her hand pulling me up from the sewing room floor, her grip stronger than I expected. She doesn't seem crazy to me.

"Where's Li?" I ask when we reach Kai, suddenly feeling nervous again. He just grins and points up to a staircase that runs along the outside of a splintering, wooden three-story building. At the top, leaning against a dangerously rickety-looking rail, Li is smiling down at us under the mostly obscured moon.

"Careful, Li," I call up automatically.

He motions for us to join him, and Jing, Kai and I tiptoe up the wobbly stairs.

My thighs ache from running, and Jing's seem to as well, because Kai passes us, taking the steps two at a time. He doesn't seem tired at all, and I wonder, again, where he and Li came from, what kind of life they've led before now.

When we reach Li on the third-story landing, Jing looks down at the ground and then up at the dark sky. She holds her hands up in the air, as if feeling wind for the first time.

Behind us is a closed wooden door. To someone's apartment? I put my finger to my lips and look around uneasily. The window next to the door is cracked open, and I can smell the lingering scent of dinner. It makes my mouth water. A dirty cat pushes its way through the window, startling us, and jumps onto the landing to wind its way around our legs. We lean against the flimsy railing.

Another gust of wind rolls over us and blows our hair off our foreheads as we stand in single file. In the distance, beyond the row of stores, the wheat stalks sway. They give way to dark rolling hills, which eventually rise steeply into looming black mountains.

At the base of the nearest mountain is a squat two-story building. Dim lights shine from within. I can see now that it seems to be composed of several different-size rectangles shoved together haphazardly. Four smokestacks of varying sizes jut upward from the roof, three of them spewing ghostly smog. On one side, a small enclosure protrudes slightly from the pink wall. Pale light seeps out of a horizontal gap where the walls should meet the roof; I recognize it immediately as the bathroom.

I look at Kai, Li, and Jing—all in dirty, stinking T-shirts, like me, and with identical haircuts. For a minute—just a quick minute—I can't believe I'm here. I feel like I'm separated from the others by a clear curtain. I can't believe the splintery, damp wood beneath my feet, or the humid wind in my hair. I can't believe that these are my companions—filthy and wise—and I can't believe *myself*, what I've survived.

Next to me, Jing shifts. Tears are running down her cheeks as she stares at the ramshackle factory in the distance. "Jing?" I ask, suddenly believing it—suddenly believing it *all*.

She turns to me. "Almost five years" is all she says, and I nod and put my hand on her shoulder.

The cat leaps onto the railing and meows until Li pets it. Somewhere above us thunder rumbles, and the moon disappears completely behind a cloud as the first raindrops hit our faces.

Chapter 14

Clara

WHEN WE LAND in Beijing, rain is splattering so hard against the plane windows that it looks like we're in a car wash. Mom and Dad edge into the aisle along with everybody else, and Dad opens the overhead bin.

Lola and I were both terrified of the car wash when we were little. I remember this one time when the two of us huddled on the floor of the backseat as soapy water slammed against the windows of Dad's car. The brushes came next. They looked like giant, evil Muppets swooping in to get us, and Lola and I screamed and cried. Dad turned around, looked down at us, and said, *I told you you could have waited inside with Mom.*

I like a challenge! Lola had sobbed, practically choking on her tears, and Dad had laughed and laughed.

I wonder what it's like in Yuming's factory when it's raining. I visualize the huge, open room that I've been picturing, rain slamming against its windows.

On the plane ride I had closed my eyes, but I had tried to stay awake while Mom and Dad whispered next to me about the reservations that the Chinese International Travel Service had made. I'd overheard Mom the day before, talking on the phone to someone named Alma. Alma must have pulled up our information from last time on her computer, because Mom had to correct her, explaining that only *one* child would be traveling with them this time. Then Mom said she had to take another call. But there was no other call.

"According to Alma, the train station in Beijing isn't sending out tickets ahead of time anymore," Mom had told Dad during the flight. "We have to pick them up at the station."

"And a sleeping car isn't available?" Dad whispered back.

"No, but we got first class. It will be fine. Remember, the seats recline?"

They whispered back and forth. Every now and then one of them nudged me and reminded me not to sleep too much. We changed planes in San Francisco and, for the rest of the journey to China, every time I opened my eyes, I could almost *see* Lola's ghost perched on Dad's armrest. *Make a plan, Clara! You have three days in Beijing, and then it's off to Shanghai. How are you going to find Yuming?*

"Try to stay up, if you can," Mom kept reminding me. "It will be close to bedtime when we arrive."

I nodded, my eyes heavy. *I'll ask around when we're there,* I imagined saying to Lola. *At the hotel, at restaurants . . . People speak English. There's gotta be someone who knows of a pink factory. I'm sure there's* someone.

Finally, Mom stopped nudging me and I fell asleep, thinking those words over and over as the plane streaked toward the country where my sister was born. *I'm sure there's someone, I'm sure there's someone, there's got to be someone.*

Now, in a cab, we make our way toward our hotel along crowded highways that turn, eventually, into small streets. Rain pounds the windows. My head is foggy with exhaustion. "What time is it here?" I ask.

"I think it's seven fifteen," Dad says. "Dinnertime, and then bedtime."

"It's eight fourteen," Mom corrects, looking at her phone. I lean my head against the window.

"Yes, eight fourteen," the cabdriver chimes in, in a heavy accent.

"Oh, you speak English?" Mom asks.

"Yes, little bit," he says, smiling at Mom and me in the rear-view mirror.

Cabdrivers! I imagine Lola shouting from the front seat. I can just imagine her up on her knees, between Dad and the driver, looking back at me. *Cabdrivers are a great place to start! You'll be taking cabs constantly!*

I press my lips together to hide my smile and close my eyes again as Mom and Dad ask him about the weather forecast and how crowded some of the tourist sites have been lately. The next thing I know, Dad is waking me up. We're in front of our hotel—the same fancy stone building where we stayed three years ago. Above the glass revolving doors, in gold glowing lights, GRAND BEIJING HOTEL flashes on and off in both Chinese characters and English.

I sit in a puffy red chair in the lobby, surrounded by our luggage, while Mom and Dad check in and exchange money. I remember running through here with Lola. We loved the carpet—the swirly yellow design on the red background. *Follow the Yellow Brick Road!* Lola had yelled, and we'd twirled around the room until Mom and Dad made us stop.

"Remember last time?" I ask Mom and Dad sleepily as we wait for the elevator. "The shower?" They both laugh a little, and I can tell they're thinking the same thing as me: I wish Lola were here, too, laughing along with us.

Lola had called first shower as soon as we got to the hotel. Maybe ten minutes after she turned on the water, she screamed for Mom and me to come into the bathroom. I remember peeking around the shower curtain in the steamy bathroom. The tub was about an inch away from overflowing. *It's a shower-bath!* Lola had said, giggling. She plopped down into the tub and sudsy water sloshed over the sides onto the fancy bathroom floor.

Lola! Mom had yelled. *Open the drain!*

There is no drain! Her hair was thick with suds, and she was laughing.

Mom reached around Lola to shut off the water while Dad called the front desk. *We'd like to move to a new room*, I remember him saying. *One that has a drain in the tub.* There was a pause. *A drain*, he said again. *You know, where the water goes down? Into the pipes?* Soon, a pretty Chinese lady knocked on the door and ushered us across the hall to our new room. Lola was wrapped in a fancy hotel robe and suds were sliding down the sides of her face.

"This time, we do a room check first," Mom announces, unlocking our door. The room is big and extravagant, just like before. Mom and Dad walk around and try out the light switches and faucets. They open and close the mini fridge and the drains before they decide that everything is in working order.

I watch them from one of the beds. I'm so tired it feels like I'm dreaming. "This room looks exactly like the one we stayed in last time," I say. Outside the window, the city lights twinkle through a curtain of rain, and I lie back on the thin pillow.

Dad tugs at my feet. "Don't go to sleep," he says. I close my eyes. "The only way to conquer jet lag is to pretend it doesn't exist. Open your eyes, Clara! Closing your eyes is the beginning of the end!"

"I'm not hungry anyway," I mumble. I'd rather just forget dinner and go to sleep. Then we can wake up in the morning and I can get to work, tracking down Yuming.

"I just need to grab a quick shower," Mom announces. "I feel gross from the planes."

I nod.

"Up, Clara, up!" Dad shouts. I can't move. Finally, he lies down next to me. "Wake me up when you're out of the shower, then," he mumbles to Mom.

Lola was way better at dealing with jet lag than me. Last time, I fell asleep in the middle of the day on a cement bench in the center of a wide-open room in the Beijing National Art Museum of China. I remember waking up and staring at the far-away ceiling, disoriented, as Lola pulled my shoes and socks off.

Lola! I remember Mom yelling.

I just wanted to see how asleep she was, Lola had whined, trying not to laugh.

"What's so funny?" Dad asks me now.

I turn my head in his direction. "Huh?" I ask.

"You were giggling."

"I was?"

"Yup."

"I guess I was having a funny dream," I say.

Mom comes out of the bathroom, her head wrapped in an orange towel. "Everybody up!" she announces. Dad stumbles into the bathroom to shave. I change my clothes, making sure to put Yuming's picture and note into the pocket of my clean jeans. As soon as Dad is ready, we ride the elevator back downstairs to the restaurant.

It's the fancy one where we always ate last time, since even fancy stuff in China barely costs anything. The hostess seats us in the back, in front of flowing red curtains with swirly gold decorations. I don't remember these curtains from before. Lola would have loved them. She would have jumped up from her seat and hidden behind them. She would have parted them and stuck just her head through and giggled. She would have done it until Mom and Dad stopped laughing long enough to tell her to quit bothering the people around us.

"Earth to Clara," Dad says. I look at him. He and Mom are already seated on one side of the table. I'm staring at the curtains.

"Someone's a little tired," Mom teases. "Me, too. If I fall asleep in my food, will somebody carry me up to the room?"

"Of course," Dad says, kissing her cheek and resting his head on top of hers. If Lola were here, she would make fake gagging noises. Dad opens the menu. He's about to start reading when he looks up, his eyes damp. "Should we still play the translation game?" he asks.

I shrug. I'm so tired.

A few months before we went to China last time, my cousins moved to Spain. Whenever we FaceTimed with them, they'd tell us about funny English translations they'd seen around Europe. Lola's favorite was one from a museum in Paris that said: QUIET! DO NOT BREAK OTHER EARS. I thought one from Seville was better—DANGER! NO YOU FALLS IN THE RIVER!

While we were in China, we took pictures of funny English translations we saw and emailed them to our cousins. You can usually find good ones on menus. During the flight home, my family voted for the funniest. It was a tie between a sign Lola saw in a park near the orphanage—NO HOOLIGANING!—and a label I found in a market: SPICEY CHICKEN PAWS. I had spotted it as we wandered past booths of flowers and plants and gross-looking raw meat. When I pointed it out to Lola, we started laughing so hard we could barely stand.

Now, I wonder how many of the Chinese words on American signs are wrong.

Mom rubs Dad's hand. "We can play that tomorrow," she says. "For now, just order anything veggie that looks familiar." She looks down at her lap and then back up at me, a small smile creeping across her face. "Unless, that is, they have spicy chicken paws."

Dad laughs and covers his face; it looks like he's laughing and crying at the same time. I wish I could just skip dinner and go upstairs. If Lola were here, maybe Mom and Dad would let us go on our own. *Straight to the room and straight to bed,* they'd say. *No fooling around!*

The waitress comes over to take our order, and Dad points to a few things on the menu. "Being here brings back so many memories," he says, wiping his eyes with his napkin when she walks away. "All of a sudden, I can't stop thinking about Lola's adoption—the first time I held her. She didn't even seem confused, you know? She seemed perfectly content when she was put into my arms—like she *knew* she belonged with me. With *us*."

Nobody says anything. "What's your earliest memory of your sister?" Dad asks me.

"Earliest?"

"Yeah. I mean, obviously Mom and I both remember her adoption like it was yesterday." As he talks, Mom looks at her lap. Her eyes are puffy, and they seem too big in her thin face. "But you don't remember that, of course," he goes on. "What's the first thing you can remember about her?"

"Um, I'm not sure," I say, searching my mind and feeling Yuming's photograph in my pocket. "I mean, I remember dropping her off somewhere with Mom, and I was so upset that she was going somewhere that I wasn't," I say. "Maybe she was starting kindergarten?"

"Preschool," Mom corrects quickly. "I bet it was preschool. Were you crying?"

"Yeah!" I say. "She was wearing blue jeans and a yellow shirt."

"With a rainbow on it?" Mom asks.

"Yeah, a rainbow, and she was walking through a door with a teacher or some lady and she stuck out her tongue at me, like 'Ha-ha, I'm going somewhere cool and you're not.'"

"That was preschool," Mom says, nodding and smiling. "You were so sad. It was probably ninety degrees that day, and she insisted on wearing those jeans." Dad is playing with the cloth napkin in front of him. Mom continues, "I think she wore them every single day that summer. They were too short on her, but she would not give them up. I have no idea what she saw in them." She takes a drink of water. "I wonder what I did with them. I should have saved them."

Dad puts the napkin down, looks at Mom, and gives her a little nod. "Clara, honey," she says, all serious, breathing in and out slowly, "your father and I—well, there was—I should say, there *is* another purpose for this trip. One we *tried* to tell you about, but . . . Well, anyway, it's something we didn't tell you about. But we need to tell you now."

I think immediately of Yuming, and, for a second, I feel dizzy with relief. *We're going to save Yuming,* I picture them saying, smiling. But they're both looking down. They're looking down, and they're not smiling. Dad wipes his eyes again as Mom opens her purse and takes out a tiny round silver box—like a jewelry box, which seems ridiculous, because why would they be giving me jewelry? I don't even *care* about jewelry. Lola—she was the more artistic one. She was the one who would have appreciated—

"Clara," Mom goes on, "we—Dad and I—we want you to take this." Slowly, I reach for the box. She presses it into my hand.

"What is it?" I ask. They're acting so weird, and I'm so tired. I'm not even hungry.

"So," Dad says, as I wrap my fingers around the box, "when your sister was cremated, Mom and I, well, we had in mind that maybe, if it felt right, maybe we'd eventually make a trip back to China. We had a small portion of Lola's ashes put into this—"

I drop the box onto the table. It clangs against an empty glass, and a family at the next table looks over at us. Lola would be disgusted. She would be so horrified to think of herself as dust in a silver box on this table. In a restaurant! In a restaurant where people eat and—

"Listen to us, sweetie," Dad goes on firmly. "Your mother and I, initially, we did it for *us*. We did it because we thought that maybe, maybe *we* would feel more comfortable if part of Lola was, eventually, back in China. But now we think"—Mom and Dad look at each other again—"now we think that having this"—Dad picks up the silver box and holds it out toward me again. I don't take it—"That having this could be more helpful for you," he finally finishes.

"We think this is something *you* need. More than us," Mom adds, wiping her eyes with her napkin again.

"What do you mean, it's something *I* need?" I ask, staring at the box. "What am I supposed to do with this?"

Mom puts her hand on top of Dad's. "We don't know," he says quietly. "But we think you'll be able to figure it out." He stares down at the table to avoid my eyes. "We think it will *help you*, to figure it out."

I flush with embarrassment. I imagine Mom and Dad whispering about me at night, when I'm asleep. *Clara needs help. She's struggling. She's suffering. She needs help.* Lola would have known how to deal with this. I feel like such an idiot.

"We want this experience of being in China again to help you process your sister's death," Mom goes on. "To help you understand and accept that she's"—she looks me in the eye—"To help you understand and accept that she's not with us anymore."

I turn my head. Before I can figure out what to say, our waitress walks toward us, smiling, with a tray.

"Here you go," she says with a heavy accent, placing several bowls of food in the center of the table. I don't want her to see the silver box, so I shove it into my pocket next to Yuming's note and picture.

Mom and Dad thank the waitress, and she bustles away. I wonder where she lives, and whether she knows of a pale-pink factory anywhere. I look around, almost like I'm searching for Lola's ghost, but all I see is the dimly lit restaurant, the tables occupied by rich-looking Chinese families on vacation. Glasses clink. The family next to us laughs. I try to ignore the silver box in my pocket and the fact that part of Lola's body is inside of it. Lola would hate that. She'd hate the whole idea of it.

Rain slams into the windows at the far side of the restaurant, and I can hear thunder rumbling. As I push some weird-looking food around on my plate with my chopsticks, I think, There's got to be *someone* in this hotel who has seen Yuming's factory. There must be someone who could tell me how to get to her. The silver box presses into my thigh so I shove it deeper into my pocket.

That's the only *thing I need from this trip.*

Chapter 15

July 6th
Hebei Province, China

Yuming

THE GRUMBLING OF my stomach is loud enough to be heard over the groans of thunder, and despite the fact that we're huddled under the awning of a closed store, I'm soaked. Massive puddles have already formed in the dirt road. The moon, visible just a little while ago, is completely hidden; it's pitch-black now.

"Well, I guess we're officially safe from Mr. Zhang," Kai says from somewhere to my left, a hint of anger in his voice. "He couldn't see *or* hear us even if he was across the street right now. We should have gone to that bar. Maybe someone would have let us stay in their home overnight if—"

"No way," I say. "That would have been stupid."

"Okay," Jing pipes in, "enough debating. What are we going to do? I'm starving."

"Me, too," Li announces.

"Yeah, me, too," I say.

There is fumbling at the doorway behind us. "Kai?" I ask quickly, spinning around.

"It's just me." He sighs. "All right, Li, where's that piece of metal I told you to put in your pocket?"

"Metal?" Jing asks.

"Here," Li says, handing it to him.

"How is a piece of metal going to—" I start to ask. The answer is the creak of a door. "Did you just open that lock?"

"I did." I can hear the smile in Kai's voice and, before I know it, a dim light from a single lamp pours out of the store, illuminating the silver raindrops in its path. "I know, I know," Kai says as Li, Jing, and I step, dripping, through the doorway and into the small grocery. "Too risky to have the light on. I agree, so let's do this quickly."

I look around at the shelves. They are packed with everything one could possibly want or need: T-shirts, paper, pens and pencils, bandages for blistered feet, Coca-Cola, cookies, Guo Dan Pi. I gawk—especially at the food.

Li is already walking down the aisle, removing a variety of items and rearranging the goods around them so as not to leave holes. Jing has found a pile of rags, and she's wiping the floor behind him.

"Here," she interrupts. "Give me your shoes, Li."

He kicks them off, and she places them on top of the rag to dry. Then she takes her own shoes off. Kai does the same before standing in the middle of the small store, barefoot, surveying the walls as if taking inventory.

"Kai," I say uncomfortably, "you look as if you're plotting a murder." I wrap my arms around my soaked body, thinking both of how hungry I am and how wrong it is to steal from the store owner.

Kai studies me in the dim light as the rain pounds on the tin roof overhead. Self-conscious, I hug myself tighter.

"Where do you come from, anyway?" he asks. He seems angry, as though he doesn't want the hassle of having to explain himself to me.

"Where do *you* come from?" I respond, suddenly defensive.

He smiles at me a little, correcting himself. "I asked you first."

I nod. "About three hours west of Shanghai."

He lets out a whistle. "Mr. Zhang got you from Shanghai? I could tell you were southern, but I didn't think he'd have gotten you from *that* far. Me and Li, we come from *all over*." He swoops his dripping arm before me, grinning proudly, as if indicating all of Hebei Province.

"Mama's in Zhao Village," Li calls over to us, "right near Beij—"

"We'll need these, I'm sure," Kai announces louder than necessary as he takes down a handful of matchbooks. I feel sorry for him. I imagine their mama—a woman walking alone, away from them, down a small country road. I swallow hard. The back of the woman looks just the way I've always imagined *my* mama.

"What will we use those for?" I ask, trying to change the subject. I feel so strange—starving, exhausted, and wide-awake, all at the same time.

He looks back at me. "I don't know yet, good girl from west of Shanghai." There is anger in his voice again, but I know it is misdirected. He's angry about his mama. He is angry that he isn't the only one in charge. I open and close my mouth. At least I had Wai Po and Wai Gong, I think. If it weren't for them, Bolin and I might have turned out just like Kai—bitter. I feel proud, but then heaviness settles in my empty, grumbling belly. Wai Po and Wai Gong are gone. Now, I *am* like Kai—maybe not bitter, but on my own.

Li comes to Kai's side and tugs on his big brother's dripping shirt. He holds a box of crackers up to him. "Your favorites, Kai-Kai."

Actually, Kai has more than I do: He has his brother. I squeeze my eyes shut, and when I open them, Kai is studying me. "You weren't there long, were you?"

"Where?" I ask, attempting to read his never-still mind.

"The factory."

"Almost three months," I say. "Not long, but long enough."

"Yeah, I could tell," Kai answers offhandedly.

"How?" My toes tingle with cold in my saturated shoes.

"Your sewing," he goes on. "It wasn't so good." He rips open the box of crackers. "So, are you hungry or not?"

I nod, looking around the dark grocery.

"Come help me, then," he says. "But first, take your shoes

off, like the rest of us. For Jing, I sense there is hope, but you—you'll need to be *taught* a thing or two, or you'll never survive on the streets."

His words startle me. *Survive on the streets?* No. I'm going to find Bolin. I *have* to find him. He and I will live at home, together, in Yemo Village. We'll return to our rice fields, to school, to . . . But words march into my mind like soldiers: *One and a half billion people in all of China. One and a half billion people. One and a half billion. It will be impossible to find one person among so many.*

Kai is waiting to give me my first lesson on how to steal—on how to *survive*. I swallow back my tears and clear my throat. I weigh my options. *You need to eat*, Wai Gong would say, nodding slightly. I measure the risks. When I get home, I could pay the store owner back, somehow. . . . And once we are fed and able to get far enough away, perhaps we can go to the police. . . .

"All right," I say. "Teach me."

☆

I hold a lit match in front of me and look around our cramped nest. We're sitting behind the sales counter in the dark, all wearing oversize, brightly colored T-shirts. Our wet clothes are spread out to dry. There is a heap of food in front of us. The flame bites at my fingers and I quickly blow it out.

I hear the rustle of packages being opened. Otherwise we eat in silence, shoving handfuls of cookies and crackers into our mouths and drinking from shared cans of Coca-Cola and bottled water. The sugary syrup from the Coca-Cola coats my teeth. I'm full, but Kai, Li and Jing are still eating, so I take another handful of crackers, not knowing when I'll have food again.

"I'm freezing," Li announces when we've finished.

"Come," Jing says to him, sounding again like Wai Po used to. "Sit with me." I lie on my back and listen to her talk. "I'll write you a message on your back," she says. I roll on my side and pull my knees up into the T-shirt, trying to get warm.

"You can write?" he asks softly.

"A few things," she says. "There was a lady at the factory a long time ago who taught me when I'd stay in the barracks at night. Her name was Ling."

I picture Jing as a little girl, entering Mr. Zhang's factory and being shoved onto a bench in front of a sewing machine. I wonder what Mr. Zhang is doing right now and picture him storming through the front door of this store. Wai Gong once told me that every hiding place should have two exits.

"I can't write a thing," Li announces proudly. "Draw me a picture instead."

"All right, then." I listen as Jing traces a design on Li's back with her finger and he tries to guess what it is. I can make out only the outline of her face and the whites of her eyes in the darkness, but I sense that she's calm, content. I suppose if I had been in that factory for five years, maybe I'd feel calm now as well.

What is next for us? Surely it would be too risky to seek help from a police officer this close to the factory. We need to leave here well before dawn and get as far away from Mr. Zhang as possible.

"Our plan," Kai announces expertly, as if reading my mind, "is to make money at tourist sites."

"Tourist sites?" Jing asks quietly.

"A wonderful place to find everything you need," Kai goes on, and Li stifles a laugh.

"Remember last time? The old man chased us after I stole his change?" he whispers. "Remember when the guard—"

"*Shh*, Li," Kai warns.

"There are many ways to make money at tourist sites," Kai continues, sounding like a teacher.

"All right, then," Jing replies quickly. "Where do you suggest?" She seems unfazed by Li's laughter and mysterious story about stealing change from somebody.

"Where else," Kai replies quickly, "but the most popular tourist destination in all of China? Badaling—the Great Wall."

Chapter 16

July 7th
Beijing, China

Clara

THE GREAT WALL of China looms in front of us, and I peer at it through the dirty window of the cab. *It's a snake! It's a massive snake made of stones!* Lola had yelled the last time we were here.

Yesterday, after Mom and Dad handed me the ashes, Lola's ghost disappeared. I'd tried to picture her—in the restaurant, in the elevator, and back in the hotel room—but she was gone, and I'd stumbled around, getting ready for bed in a daze. I felt like the black hole might come for me, so I tucked Yuming's picture and note into the little pocket in my pajama pants to keep it away.

But when I woke up this morning, I could see Lola again, sitting on the foot of my bed, grinning at me, and I'd laid back and looked up at the ceiling in relief. Her image followed us around—to the hotel's breakfast buffet, which she used to love;

through the narrow, winding streets of the neighborhood; to Dad's favorite dumpling restaurant for lunch.

Now I think for a second of the silver tin that I left in the bedside table in our hotel room, and I touch the edge of Yuming's photograph in my pocket. This driver speaks a little English, and I'm hoping that if I take my time getting out of the cab at the Great Wall, I'll have a chance to ask him if he's ever seen a pink factory somewhere outside of Beijing.

The cab slows as it passes under a blue-and-green archway and pulls into the giant parking lot that is crowded with rows of tour buses, city buses, cabs, and cars. The smell of exhaust drifts through the cracked windows. Off to our right are the ticket office and the street that's lined with millions of stands and shops selling all kinds of souvenirs. The smoggy, white sky feels too low to the ground.

Down the road I see the Starbucks that we decided last time has the best bathroom in China, and the stone archway that leads to the entrance to the Great Wall. Up in the hills, the massive stone snake is packed with people. It winds up and down the green slopes. The rain stopped overnight, and the exhaust from the cabs and buses mixes with the smell of wet dirt. Everything seems greener than I remember it.

When our cab finally pulls over to the side of the parking lot, Mom hands the driver some money.

"Thank you," he says.

I picture Yuming in her factory, take a breath, and drop my elastic bracelet onto the floor of the cab.

"Okay, everybody out," Mom announces, shoving her wallet into her fanny pack and opening the door.

I let her and Dad slide out before calling to them. "Wait a sec. My bracelet fell off. It's somewhere on the floor."

The cabdriver turns around and smiles at me with a mouth full of broken teeth.

"What's that, honey?" Mom asks, turning back to the cab.

"Oh, um, my bracelet. I dropped it. I'll be right there."

"Sorry," Mom says to the cabdriver, who is still watching me. "She'll just be a minute." She holds up one finger, like she's making sure he understands.

"A minute, yes," he says, nodding.

I crouch on the floor as Mom says something to Dad and whisper to the cabdriver. "Do you know of any factories in Beijing?"

He twists around even farther, so he's almost facing the backseat now. "Factory?"

"Yeah, you know, where people make things."

"Factory, yes, many in Beijing."

"Have you seen a pink one?"

"Pink?"

"Yeah," I say, picking up my bracelet. I point to the pink rubber bands on it, still watching Mom out of the corner of my eye. "This color. Pink."

"Very nice," he says, smiling wider. "Very pretty jewelry."

"Everything okay?" Mom asks, poking her head back into the open cab door. I sigh.

"Yup, found it." I inch out of the backseat as the cabdriver waves to me. I force myself to smile, close the car door, and walk over to Mom and Dad. They have stepped away from the crowd to look through the brochure that the concierge at the hotel gave them.

I'd showered quickly this morning and told Mom and Dad that I'd meet them in the lobby. When I was alone, I'd asked the man at the front desk if he had a list of all the factories in the area. Maybe I could figure out a way to call them. I could ask for someone who speaks English. I could tell them I was an American student doing a project on buildings in China. I could ask them . . . I could ask them if their factory was pink.

But when I told the concierge that I needed a phone book, he looked confused. "I'm sorry, but we do not have this kind of book," he told me.

I nodded, backing away, and sat in the puffy red chair to wait for Mom and Dad. My mind raced. *Just keep asking around!* I heard Lola saying. *You still have three days!*

Now, in the parking lot, a family of Americans pushes past me on their way to the Great Wall. A little girl who looks about five is crying and whining that her feet hurt. I smile at her, but she keeps crying.

Dad is pointing to something in the brochure, and Mom is digging through her fanny pack for the tickets that Alma ordered for us ahead of time. Lola would have rolled her eyes at their fanny packs, and we all would have laughed. I sigh and watch a city bus pull in next to a double-decker tour bus. The city bus honks, and I notice some sort of commotion aboard. Mom and Dad are still trying to figure something out. The bus driver opens the doors and stands up. I see him yelling and gesturing toward the back of the bus. Suddenly, four of the windows open and, at the exact same moment, four kids jump out—one from each window. They have identical haircuts and are wearing brightly colored T-shirts that are way too big on them. I wonder if they're siblings. One of them has a tan sack with him. He lands funny when he drops from the window and yelps as he twists his ankle. Another helps him up. The smallest one laughs as all four of them disappear into the crowds.

The bus driver pushes through the mob that has gathered at the door to the bus. He spins in a circle, looking for the kids, but they're gone. With so many people here, there's no way he'll find them, and I smile a little. Lola would have loved seeing that. She would have cheered the kids on. *Go! Run faster!* she would have screamed, until Mom and Dad told her to stop.

"Okay, Clara, this way," Dad says. I follow him and Mom down the main road leading to the Wall, past the beggars, the tour groups, and the Chinese women carrying colorful umbrellas to block the sun. I trail behind them, thinking about Lola.

Last time, Mom and Dad had made us promise to hold hands with each other until we were back in the cab. Even

Lola, who was always so brave, was freaked out by the crowds. It was true that I'd never seen so many people in one place in my entire life.

Lola had a necklace made of rubber bands—just like the bracelet I'd dropped on purpose in the cab—and she'd taken it off her neck and looped it around my right wrist and her left one. *This way, even if we're not holding hands, we won't get separated!* she'd announced, proud of her idea. I still remember how it felt to be attached to her for hours.

We pass the fancy Starbucks and the big rock with BADALING written on it in red Chinese characters, and we climb the steep steps to the Great Wall. Mom is walking ahead of Dad, who is walking ahead of me. Each step is so narrow that I can barely fit my whole foot on it.

Last time, as Mom and Dad walked ahead of Lola and me, we swung our connected hands back and forth and looked for funny signs. Lola found one at the entrance that said NO LOUDING! We'd giggled as Mom snapped a photo of it. Along the Great Wall I found a sign that warned NO PERMITTING JUMPS! NO PERMITTING CLIMBING! NO PERMITTING BATHROOM! and we pointed to it, laughing, and called for Mom to take its picture, too. We stretched the rubber band necklace as far is it could go as we walked along. Lola tried to climb the side of the Wall with only one free hand until Mom and Dad made her stop. *No permitting climbing,* Dad had teased. There was a man with a puppy, begging for money, and the puppy had chewed on our fingers while we pet it. There was a family, also begging, playing weird-looking guitars. Lola wanted to give them all money, and Mom let us, until she ran out of coins. We had walked for what seemed like forever, Mom and Dad holding hands ahead of us, as the crowds gradually thinned out.

Now, it's pretty much the same, except that everything is different. I walk alone behind Mom and Dad. We pass people taking pictures, more beggars, and a little Chinese girl in a tutu. There's a man dressed in rags with a dirty, gray dog, and I wonder if it's the same dog that chewed on my fingers two years ago. I pretend Lola is with me so I don't feel so alone.

Last time, when we got this far, Lola and I were playing Rock, Paper, Scissors. I think of it for the first time in forever. *Rock, Paper, Scissors, shoot!* Lola and I would scream. The sun was getting low in the sooty sky over the hills, just like it is now. It was so weird because, as Lola and I were walking along, our wrists connected by her necklace, we tied seventeen times in a row. I still can't believe it.

We pass the four kids who escaped from the bus windows. They're jogging down the path, and I hope the bus driver is long gone by now.

I mean, how could two people tie in Rock, Paper, Scissors seventeen times in a row? It seems almost impossible. *Rock, Paper, Scissors, shoot!* Both rock. *Rock, Paper, Scissors, shoot!* Both scissors. *Rock, Paper, Scissors, shoot!* Both paper. Again and again and again—seventeen times—until Lola's scissors cut my paper, and she won.

Mom and Dad stop ahead of me and I watch them look over the side of the wall, toward the cloudy sunset where the sky is weird and hazy and pink. The smog is thickening, making the breeze feel heavy and dense.

My heartbeat quickens as I realize that our first day is just about over. I force my thoughts away from Lola. I haven't accomplished *anything* to get us closer to Yuming. In just two days, we'll be leaving Beijing. I lean against the wall and reach my hand into my pocket. The edges of Yuming's photograph are so worn by now that they're soft—just like the original I gave to Susan Zhau. I only have two more full days to figure out how to get to Yuming—and if I don't find her by then, I never will.

Chapter 17
July 7th–8th
Beijing, China

Yuming

NOW I KNOW. Now I know why Kai had insisted on stuffing a huge sack from the market full of food. It was practically more than we could carry, but he insisted on bringing it with us when we slipped out of the store well before dawn.

Here at the Great Wall, the sun has almost set in the misty, pink sky behind us; it's nothing but a thin orange line above the hills, and standing in front of us are a cast of frightening-looking characters who, a few months ago, I would have shuddered to be near. But now I jut my chin forward, like Kai does, so I look unafraid.

Kai is holding a box of candies out to a bearded man with broken teeth who, at Kai's insistence, we'd spent the greater part of the afternoon looking for. The man is dressed in rags, and a mangy gray dog sits, panting, at his feet. "One box?" the man asks Kai sharply. "One box for three people, for the week?" He laughs, but as if to say that he finds nothing funny about it.

"It's all I have," Kai lies. Off to the side, hidden in the shadows of the Wall, Li is pretending to sleep, his arms wrapped around the bulky sack of bottles and boxes like it's a giant stuffed toy. The old man looks from Kai, to me, to Jing. I don't blink.

The man snatches the box from Kai's hand and laughs again, but this time like he *is* amused. "One box is nothing." He rips it open and pours its contents out at his feet. The dog smiles up at him before wolfing the candy down.

We are on a hill off to the side of the Wall. A teenage boy who has been watching us from beneath a tree takes a few steps toward the old man's back, ogling the dog and the slobbery candy, until the man pivots swiftly, as if he has eyes in the back of his head, and pulls a knife from his pocket. "Get back, Tao," he hisses, and the teenager throws his head back and roars with laughter before disappearing into the shadows.

I keep my chin high and try to breathe evenly. Why couldn't Tao have been Bolin? Why can't my brother suddenly appear and take me away from here?

The man turns to face us again. I eye Kai and Jing. They're still staring at him, just like Kai had told us to do when he'd explained his plan.

"Kai-Kai—last time, you brought me more," the man says. "And where's that little runt of yours?"

Kai doesn't answer.

The old man leans toward us. He smells like something rotten. "I need more. Three people for a week? The price for that is *more*."

Kai stares at the man for another moment before finally gesturing to Li, who jumps up and drags the sack over.

"Ah, the runt *is* here! The runt whose boldness got me in trouble last time."

Li grins up at the filthy man proudly as the man snatches the sack from his hand. Startled, Li slowly backs up until he's at his brother's side.

"If you have the runt with you, you can forget it."

"Then give me back my food." I can tell that Kai is trying to keep his voice steady, but it's wavering. If we can't stay here, near this portion of wall that the rotting old man says he *owns*, then where? It had taken us hours to get from the tiny village to the Great Wall today. We had waited and waited in the shadows near a gas station before sneaking onto a bus when the driver got out to fuel up and pay. When the bus reached a larger town, we leaped from its windows, made our way to a bus station, and stowed away on a different coach. Now it's practically dark out. We are exhausted and dirty. We have nowhere else to go.

The old man laughs and laughs until he can barely stand. The gray dog wags its tail, smiling and panting at its owner. The man looks us over again before he digs through the sack, nodding. Then his face turns serious. "This food is mine. I will give you permission to stay: four people, including runt, one night. When the sun comes up, I want you gone. And I don't *ever* want to see you again. You are trouble."

Kai looks as if he is going to protest, as though he's going to tell the old man what he told us as we huddled together behind the store counter last night: *The Great Wall is the best place to beg and pickpocket.*

I had been wary, thinking, It's possible that Mr. Zhang could look for us there; it might even be the first place he would go. But I didn't say anything.

Can we stay there through the winter again? Li had mumbled. He was close to sleep.

Through the winter, Kai had agreed before turning on his side, his back toward Jing and me. *There are people—a whole group—they live there behind the Wall, all year long.*

I had nodded as he talked, promising to teach us how to survive, but the whole time I was listening to Wai Gong's voice in my mind. *Go with them, Yuming,* I imagined him saying, his hands clasped behind his back, his face thoughtful. *You'll get enough money for a train ticket to Shanghai and a bus ticket to Yemo Village, and then you'll be on your way home.*

"This is my Wall," the old man goes on, urging me back to the present. He reaches down to pet his dog gently before looking back to us with squinting eyes. "Understand? My. Great. Wall."

Kai nods, looking defeated. The old man tosses him a box of crackers and a can of soda from the sack, and walks away.

Nearby, a fire crackles in a metal tub. It's getting cold, so we sit next to it, on the opposite side from where the smoke is blowing. Li curls into Jing's lap, and I stare at the orange flames as Kai opens the crackers. When I close my eyes, the flames are blue on the inside of my lids. Kai shoves some crackers into his mouth and passes the box to Jing. He holds the end of a stick into the hottest part of the flame until an ember glows at the end. Then he jams the ember into the rim of the metal tub. Sparks fly. One lands on my ankle, and I swat it away and cross my legs underneath myself. "Watch it, *Kai-Kai*," I taunt, suddenly so exhausted that I am angry. I didn't survive everything I've survived just to be burned alive by a miniature con artist in the hills next to the Great Wall of China.

I scoot backward, untie the white T-shirt from the factory from around my waist, and lean against the Wall, using the shirt as a cushion for my head. The stone stabs me through the thin fabric. Jing lifts Li onto Kai's lap and joins me. I think she's going to say something, but she just settles herself next to me. Soon she is asleep, her head bobbing until it is finally resting on my shoulder.

Up above, people laugh and talk. Bottles clink. I remember the stories that Mr. Chen, our teacher, told us of the Great Wall. *If you love somebody, lock a padlock on the chain at the Wall; your love will last forever.* He showed us drawings of men constructing the Wall in the olden days. He taught us how much money the Chinese government makes from wealthy tourists who pay to visit.

Wealthy tourists like the ones we saw today as Kai, Li, Jing, and I jogged west then east again along the Wall, searching for the old man with the dog. I had scanned the crowds for

Mr. Zhang as we wove our way through people from many different places: the wealthy Chinese families, the South Koreans laughing and taking pictures of one another, the American girl in sunglasses and a baseball cap who seemed lost in thought, playing Scissors, Rock, Cloth discreetly with herself, probably hoping nobody would notice.

Bolin and I had played that same game. Sometimes, there would be the longest stretch of ties—*Scissors, Rock, Cloth*. Both rock. *Scissors, Rock, Cloth*. Both scissors. *Scissors, Rock, Cloth*. Both cloth.

Where are you, Bolin?

Sleep blurs the edges of my mind. I feel myself drifting off, even though I don't think it's a good idea. *Measure your risks, Yuming*. The T-shirt is the closest thing to a pillow that I've had since leaving home to search for Bolin. The fire crackles somewhere to my right, and the voices overhead on the Wall are quieter now. *I'll just close my eyes for a minute. Tomorrow— tomorrow, it all starts. Somehow, I'll get some money. Beginning tomorrow, I'll do whatever it takes to return home.*

☆

When I open my eyes, my stomach aching with hunger, the sun is bursting through the hazy white sky. I'm leaning against the stone wall with a kink in my neck. My behind is numb and damp with dew. I look beside me to see if Jing is awake, only to find that she is gone.

Chapter 18.

Clara

WE WALK OUT of the hotel into the thick morning haze. Even though the breakfast buffet at our hotel is awesome, Mom read in her guidebook that the breakfast in the hotel around the corner is even better. So we cross the street that's crowded with bikers, honking cars, trucks, and tractors, and round the corner to the Red Dragon Hotel. Inside, a young lady directs us to the restaurant, where Mom asks for a table for three.

A hostess who speaks perfect English seats us. I watch her walk away as Mom and Dad sit down. Then I clear my throat and shove my hand into the pocket with Yuming's photograph and note. "I'm going to go find the bathroom."

Mom looks around the restaurant. "Want me to come with you?"

"No, that's okay," I say with a forced smile. "I'll ask the hostess." I leave quickly before Mom can get up to join me. I know she and Dad don't think that I'm okay, and they don't want to leave me alone. But the truth is, ever since I realized we needed to come back to China, I've felt almost as good as when Lola was alive.

At the front of the restaurant, the hostess is standing behind a tall wooden stand, talking on a cell phone. I look behind me, toward our table and the giant buffet behind it. I can't see Mom and Dad from here. *Interrupt her! Hurry!* I can hear Lola yelling. I can practically see her jumping up and down with excitement.

"Excuse me?"

The hostess moves the phone away from her ear and smiles at me. "Can I help you?"

"Yeah, um . . ." I look behind me again. "I'm wondering if you can help me with something. Because your English is really good." Lola is leaning forward, tucking her hair behind her ears, and motioning for me to move it along.

"One moment," the hostess says, then she speaks some Chinese into the phone and laughs before hanging up and turning to me. "What can I help you with?"

"We're American."

"Yes?"

"And I have a project for school."

"School," she repeats. "Yes?"

"I'm doing a project on factories in Hebei Province."

"Oh," she says, still smiling. "What kind of factories?"

Pink factories! I picture Lola yelling. I clear my throat. "Well, um, you know, any kinds."

Purses, dummy!

"Purses," I say. "On purse factories."

"Many factories make purses here in Beijing. They ship all over the world."

"Yeah, right!" I say. "Do you know of any?"

"My cousin used to work at one. She made purses and other things, too. Very hard work."

I nod. "Yeah! I know—"

"Very little sleep, and poor working conditions."

Interview! You want to interview her cousin!

"Does your cousin live around here? Maybe I could interview her!" I say, without really thinking.

"No," the hostess says sadly, tilting her head to the side. "She lives in the country now, in a small village, with her family."

I check over my shoulder and spot Mom walking my way, waving. "Have you ever seen a pink factory?" I blurt out to the hostess.

"Pink?"

"Yeah, a few hours outside of Beijing?"

"Outside of Beijing?"

Mom is getting closer.

"Huh, perhaps. . . . I come from north of here. There are many factories in the northern area—in the countryside. That's where most factories are, in fact."

"Really? In the north?"

"Yes, almost all factories in Hebei Province are in the area north of the city of Beijing."

"Great!" I say as Mom approaches.

"You find the bathroom, sweetie?" she asks.

"The bathroom is up the stairs," the woman says. "We have Western-style bathrooms. Very nice," she adds.

"I'll join you, then," Mom says, putting her arm around me.

North of the city. *My first major lead.* I congratulate myself as Mom and I walk up the stairs. Mom smiles down at me—but it's a sad kind of smile, so I look away.

At the top of the staircase, Mom stops and takes a breath. I imagine Lola standing by the bathroom door, waiting for us. I can picture her looking back and forth from my face to Mom's. "So, have you decided anything?" Mom asks me quietly.

"What do you mean?"

"About the ashes." She clears her throat. "About Lola's ashes."

I swallow hard and look away from her, to the bathroom door. The image of Lola vanishes.

"What do you mean?" I ask again, suddenly thinking of her funeral. Everyone was there. People I'd never even met were crying and blowing their noses. I was sitting in the front row between Mom and Dad, and I imagined what Lola would say if she could see what was going on. She'd roll her eyes at all the drama. She'd motion for me to sneak out the side door with her. It was a beautiful day in May.

I squeeze my eyes shut in the dim upstairs hallway of the restaurant, and then open them, trying to make the image of

Lola reappear. But I can't, and I suddenly feel panicky, as though maybe the black hole followed us to China after all. I even look around a little bit to see if Lola moved somewhere else, even though I know it's ridiculous; I know she's not *really* here.

At the funeral, I had told Mom and Dad that I couldn't do it—I couldn't be there—and I went outside. There was this huge magnolia tree at the cemetery. Lola was obsessed with magnolias. I didn't love them like she did. All you have to do is give a branch a tiny shake and all the petals fall down on your head, and that's so annoying.

But that's what I did at the funeral, while people like my cousins from Spain, Lola's teachers, and even her friends gave speeches about her. I stood under the magnolia tree and shook the branches. It was crazy how easily the petals fell off.

Mom puts her hand on my back. "I mean, have you decided if there's a special place you'd like to spread Lola's ashes?"

I can't talk for a second. *Spread them?* I stashed the tin in my backpack today—I didn't want anything to happen to it at the hotel. But I don't want to spread the ashes *anywhere*. "No," I mumble. "Not yet."

Mom nods sadly, takes my hand, and pushes open the door that says WOMEN in Chinese and in English. The bathroom is fancy, with marble tiles, and pale-green paper towels arranged on the counter in the shape of a fan. It's even better than the one at the Starbucks at the Great Wall.

"Dad and I want you to take your time," Mom says. We stand side by side in the mirror, and I watch her talk. We look alike—light-brown hair, blue eyes; so different from Lola, but I never thought about things like that. I never cared. "You know, we're going to the Dan Temple today."

I nod. Why is she telling me this? Of *course* I know that. We talked about it last night and again this morning before we left the hotel.

"Lola loved it there."

"Yeah," I say. I remember last time we hopped around on the stone floor in the courtyard. *If you step on a crack, you're dead!* Lola had yelled. We'd giggled at the Buddhas with their fat bellies, while Mom and Dad told us to shush.

Mom considers me for another minute and then finally says, "Okay, I'll be right out," stepping into a stall. "We'll have to have a quick breakfast," she goes on, through the closed door. "It's going to take a while to get to the temple. It's not even in Beijing. It's in Sunma, which is quite a ways north of the city."

"North?" I ask, smiling a little.

"Yeah. Dad asked our waitress—she said with traffic, it will probably take two hours to get there. We have to go straight north, all the way into the countryside of Hebei Province."

Suddenly, Lola is back. She grins at me from where she's sitting on the edge of the counter, and I grin back. *North of the city*, she mouths, and I nod—at the image of her and at my reflection in the mirror. Today could be the day—the day that I figure out a way to save Yuming.

Chapter 19

Yuming

TWO YEARS AGO, after Bolin moved to Shanghai, our home was strangely quiet. I missed his thumping footsteps and his easy laugh. Above the bed, tacked to the wall, was the large map of China that he had often stood in front of, studying.

As the months rolled by, Bolin had sent us money—first from Shanghai, and then from different places, and never with a return address. I had tried to picture him working, talking with new friends, playing xiangqi in parks, sleeping *somewhere* at night—but I couldn't. How could I, when I didn't even know where he was? He didn't *want* us to know where he was, and this understanding burned in my veins.

That was the beginning—the beginning of the *looking*. Everywhere I went, I searched faces, scoured crowds. I hunted for his familiar twinkling eyes and his spiky cowlick.

Like his father, Wai Po would grumble. *Abandoning his family.*

Wai Gong would correct her. *No, just an adventurer,* he'd say.

It had made me wonder about the parents I'd never known. Whenever I tried to visualize the face of the woman I imagined to be my mama, all I could see was the back of her, walking alone down the dirt road—away from me. Now, my heart thudding as I look at the empty space where Jing had slept, I am overcome by a familiar understanding: A person can be here, and then, the next moment, they can be gone.

Panicking won't do me any good, but I can't help it. I stand and turn in a quick circle, searching the area for Kai, for Li, but mostly, for Jing. I can't blame her for leaving me. I abandoned her first, after all. Is this how she had felt when she'd overheard us planning our escape in the sewing room? When Li had fallen to the cafeteria floor, clutching his stomach and moaning? When Kai and I had helped walk him to the bathroom? Am I just like my mama? My papa? Bolin?

I stumble forward, disoriented. The Wall is shrouded in morning fog. Birds chirp lethargically in the dark trees. The fire pit from last night is nothing but a tin of ash now. The sights and sounds around me are of empty spaces—of things that have ended, of people who have left. Where is Jing?

My back and neck are stiff; my red T-shirt and the seat of my pants are soaked with dew. I have a sense of dread that's different from what I felt when Mr. Zhang pushed me onto the bus. It's like the emptiness after Bolin left—a yawning space bigger than the sprawling map of China over the bed.

I duck into a crevice to change into my dry T-shirt—the white one from the factory. Then I pause. It will be easier for Mr. Zhang to spot me and recognize me in this. I'm being careless. My mind is murky from a poor night's sleep. I pull the damp red shirt over the white one and instinctively wipe the dirt off my pants.

I look left, then right, but it's difficult to see through my tears. I cannot escape the *chug, chug, chugging* of my heart—the sound of fear, of sewing machines, of trains racing away from me. Where are Kai and Li? Where is Jing?

Where is Bolin?

A repetitive scraping sound echoes softly near the Wall. I take a breath and walk quickly to the steps we took down from the Wall yesterday. Leaning against the Wall a few meters from the steps is the old man, his gray dog at his side. He's sharpening a knife on a stone in his hand, drawing the edge of the blade rhythmically across the rock over and over. As I watch him, my foggy brain clears. I hope the others are somewhere safe.

"You are all alone, I see," the man calls to me, his voice slicing through the mist. He grins at the rock and his knife as he speaks. The dog barks and wags its tail at its master. I don't say anything, but Wai Gong's voice weaves its way into my mind. *Weigh your options, Yuming.* I start to back away from him, making my way to the steps in a wide arc. The old man doesn't look at me. "Your friends—where are they?" My stomach clenches, and I wonder if he knows the answer. *Measure the risk.*

I don't respond.

Up above, on the Great Wall, I hear men's voices talking and laughing too loudly, but here, down on the moist ground, it's only this man, his dog, and me. I inch closer to the steps.

"Where are you off to?" the man asks, feeling the edge of his knife with his thumb.

I hold my chin up, as I learned from Kai. "I need to find my friends," I say boldly, still slowly moving toward the steps while keeping my eyes on the man. I'll have to pass in front of him to reach them. The dog trots over to me and sniffs my ankles. I want to run, but I don't.

"How do you know you'll find them on the Wall?" the man asks, putting down the rock but not the knife and finally looking up at me. I stop, careful not to look away from his dead eyes, his gray hair, and broken, yellow teeth.

"What do you mean?" I ask, trying to appear calm.

"Perhaps they're already on their way out."

"Out?"

"Only one night. I told you yesterday."

"Yes, but . . ." I falter. The grass appears to be moving all of a sudden, like it's the swirling river where Wai Gong taught me to fish the day after Bolin left home.

"Unless . . ." the man says, pushing himself off the Wall, "unless you want to stay on your own." He takes a step toward me. "The runt and his brother, I won't have. But I never said anything about you. And the other girl."

My eyes flit from the man's dangerous smile to his knife and back again. For a second—just one quick second—my feet won't move, but then they obey my urge and run. I race toward the stairs, the gray dog following me, barking. I could easily outrun the old man if he tried to chase me, and he knows that; he *must* know that. The dog is another matter.

I leap up the stone steps, two at a time, and dart left on the Wall. The sun is trying to break through the haze, and thin groups of tourists are already beginning to make their way along the great, snaking structure. I dodge them as I run, not looking back. Behind me, I can hear the gray dog's bark fading.

When I feel I'm a safe distance from the man, I slow to a quick walk. With each step, I search the crowd frantically—for Mr. Zhang's face, for Kai and Li, for Bolin, out of instinct. But mostly, I search for Jing. If Kai and Li have left, that's okay, I tell myself, though I'm not sure I believe it. But Jing—the thought of Jing being gone forces me into a trot again.

Sharp pains shoot up my shins from all of my running since our escape yesterday, but I don't slow down. I'll continue toward the main entrance, I think. I *have* to come across Jing. They wouldn't have left me. I push past a large crowd of Korean tourists and glance at every single face before me. Jing could not have left me the way that Bolin did.

Could he have been angry with me?

During harvest season, Bolin and I would ask to accompany Wai Gong to town to deliver the rice crop to the waiting trucks. *Yuming can come,* Wai Gong had said the last time we were all together. *She has kept up beautifully with her studies. But what about you, Bolin? What about your schoolwork?* Bolin had hung his head, and my heart had flooded with pity.

I understand why Bolin might have resented Wai Gong sometimes. And perhaps even me. . . .

If only Bolin knew that after he left home, I became distracted from my studies. I'd race through my schoolwork whenever Wai Po or Wai Gong needed to make a trip into town. I'd squint into passing cars as we rumbled along in Wai Gong's tractor. I'd peer into restaurants and bars, shops and hotels once we'd arrived in town. I'd look around frantically, just as I'm doing now.

I run faster. I need to find Jing.

Ahead of me, a guard traverses the Wall, and I look away when his eyes meet mine. Could he be under the Zhangs' control, too? It seems unlikely, but I don't want to risk it. A hot breeze lifts my sweaty hair off the back of my neck and I stop running for a moment to catch my breath. I squeeze my eyes shut at the thought of what Mr. Zhang would do if he caught us. But then I open them again, not wanting to miss anything. I lean, panting, against the Wall.

A kind-looking young couple smiles at me before the man and woman glance at each other, and suddenly I realize how I must appear to them—with my short, filthy hair; my damp, dirty clothing; the sweat running off my face. The woman opens her purse. *Ask them for help!* a voice within me screams. *They look kind! Tell them your story! Explain everything!*

I open my mouth to speak, but then I remember Mr. Zhang's pale arm shoving me onto the bus. Punching me when I lunged for the open window. Twisting my arm behind me as he said, *You are mine. You are mine, now.*

I can't trust complete strangers.

The woman holds some bills in front of me and I swallow hard. "Take this," she says, coming closer. I look down at a weed peeking up between the stones of the Wall. "Come on, now."

I step forward, feeling like the old man's gray dog. "Thank you," I whisper, staring at the bills in her hand. It is a huge amount—two hundred yuan—and I try not to let my mixed emotions show. It could be half of what I need for a ticket to Shanghai! Still, my hand won't move. I can't make myself reach for it.

"Spend it on food," she continues. "You look hungry. Or on a place to sleep. Don't spend it on . . . liquor or anything."

I'm not a beggar! I want to say. Instead I just nod and mumble "Thank you" again as she pushes the bills into my still-paralyzed hand.

I stand there, sweating, as the couple walks away into the thickening crowd.

I am a stone in a river of people; they part around me, the rock of a girl.

Chapter 20

Clara

"THERE'S THE GREAT Wall again," Dad announces from the front seat of the cab as we merge onto a busy, slow-moving highway. Through the window, I can see it winding across green hills in the distance. My eyes feel heavy and I want to close them, but I can't miss anything—this could be my chance to spot the factory.

"So, it's, like, two hours to the temple?" I ask.

"Seems like it," Mom says.

"And we're taking this highway all the way there?" I ask. Mom smiles at me. "What?" I ask her.

"You're just growing up, is all," she says, rubbing my knee.

"Yeah." I look away, thinking of Lola and how she won't be able to. I open my backpack and the inner compartment, where I stashed my city maps. I pull out the one of city streets and stare at it, but I can't make sense of anything. "Does anyone know where we are?" I ask, holding the map out to Mom. Dad glances back at us as Mom takes it and turns it around a few times. In the rearview mirror, the cabdriver looks back at me and says something in Chinese.

I shrug. He reaches down as he drives and hands a big, folded map back to me. "Thank you," I say.

He says something else, but I have no idea what, so I just smile at him again before unfolding the giant map of Beijing.

"English," he says. "Yes?"

I look down at the map. "Oh, it's in English," I say. "Thank you!"

"That's great," Mom says, inching closer to me. She points to a green area at the bottom labeled CUIJIAN PARK. "That's the park around the corner from our hotel," she says. "I think we must be on Highway 612." With her finger she traces the thick, gray road that runs the length of the map.

"Yeah," Dad adds from the front seat. "We are. That's what the hostess at the restaurant told me."

I draw my finger up from the bottom of Beijing to the top.

"Can I see for a sec?" Mom asks, and I hand her the map. "Yeah, up here is the Dan Temple," she says, pointing. "That's Sunma."

Based on what the hostess said, there's a decent chance that the factory is somewhere near where we're headed. While Mom and Dad nap, I check the map for factories, but there aren't any indicated. I trace the highway on the map with my finger, looking up every minute or so to be sure I don't miss anything. The cabdriver looks up at me in his rearview mirror from time to time.

In the distance, I can see smokestacks, but I can't make out much about the buildings they're attached to. They're far away, but none appear to be pink. The haze thins out as we bounce along and by the time we get off the highway, the air is clear. We drive through a tiny, run-down village that I can't remember from last time, and then wind along a narrow road that runs through the hills until Sunma appears, like magic, in front of us. Dan Temple stands on a hill in the center of the city.

"We're here," I whisper. Mom smiles at me.

The cabdriver pulls up next to the temple, across from a giant park. I unpeel my thighs from the vinyl seats. Mom has already folded the cabdriver's map neatly, and she hands it to me to return to him. Dad pays, and he and Mom get out on the passenger side as I pass the map through the cabdriver's window. He opens it back up, turns it around a few times like's looking for something, and then refolds it. He pushes it back toward me, smiling.

"You," he says, nodding. He points to an area it's now folded open to. "Here." His eyes are twinkly, and he seems like a grandpa, someone who lives with his kids and grandkids and tells everyone stories about what life was like when he was a boy.

I don't know what to say, so I just point to myself. "For me?"

He nods again. "You."

"Thank you," I say, unzipping my backpack and putting it inside the big pocket. "Thanks a lot."

"Yes." He starts to roll up the window but then stops. "Good luck on your journey." He closes the window all the way. I step back and he pulls away. I watch him go before I swing my backpack over my shoulders and walk over to Mom and Dad.

"What did he say to you?" Dad asks.

I smile to myself. "Just to have a good trip." He puts his arm around me, and we walk toward the entrance to the temple.

"God, I remember these," Mom says, massaging her thighs as we climb the steep stone steps. "This staircase is a doozy."

Lola would have rolled her eyes at me and mouthed, *Doozy?* Then she would have hugged Mom and raced me to the red, layered temple at the top. We would have waited there, panting, until Mom and Dad made it up.

But now, I trudge along next to Mom and Dad. I think about the cabdriver and how he wished me luck on my journey, as if he knew I was doing something important. I touch Yuming's photo in my pocket. We could be so close to her. . . .

So let's get on it! Lola would say if she were here. *You have to ask around again!*

The layers of curved red roof reflect the sky and make the area near the entrance to the temple glow in a weird pinkish light. A bunch of people are gathered around a tin trough, watching sticks of incense burn. I hate the smell of it. Inside the temple, it's cool and musty smelling.

Up ahead, in the courtyard, is the giant Buddha that Lola and I had giggled at two years ago. I remember, again, skipping around with her. *Only step on the stones, Clara,* she had warned. *The cracks mean certain death!*

I wander over to the statue, Mom and Dad following. Three beggars are sitting near the Buddha, who doesn't look funny to me anymore, only happy and kind.

"Lola really liked this place," Dad says, and I turn to him. He's gazing up at the arched roof, around at the stone columns, and into open doorways to gardens and hills. A few tour groups file into the temple behind us, and gradually people fan out around us. Soon the courtyard is filled with the sounds of footsteps and whispers.

Mom looks at me. "She loved the little ponds out back with the koi fish, and also the rock garden," she reminds me. But she doesn't need to. I get what she's hinting at, and I touch the round box of ashes in my pocket for a second.

"I know," I say, looking away. The idea of throwing Lola's ashes into a pond of fish is the most insane thing I've ever heard. Why would I *ever* do that if what I want is to have Lola right here with me, where she belongs? Anyway, those goldfish aren't the reason Lola loved the pond.

We walk around slowly. While Mom and Dad study the building, I look at the smaller Buddha statues lining the walls. Dad is much quieter than he was last time we were here, and his shoulders are stooped; it's like the black hole is just a step behind him.

Two years ago, he was completely obsessed with the architecture. He kept pointing out the *use of color* and the *perspective* and the *different historical influences*. Lola and I got sick of hearing about it all. Dad took loads of pictures for his social studies classes while we moaned. I was starving and my feet were killing me. I remember it so clearly. . . .

☆

I'm dying! Lola said, stumbling into me and practically pushing me into a passing tourist. We started laughing.

We apologize! Mom called to the person before turning to us. *Girls!*

We're dying of boredom, I told her.

Dying, Lola emphasized.

Okay, Mom said. *We'll meet you in front of the giant Buddha in thirty minutes. Not one minute later, okay?*

Lola I looked at each other. *For real?* Lola asked.

I think we can trust you, Mom said. *You have to stay inside the temple. No going out to the gardens. And, obviously, stay together.* I looked at my watch, and we skipped off.

We jumped from stone to stone. We walked from one corner of the temple to the other, never touching a crack in the floor. We made fun of Mom and Dad and their obsession with the architecture. Lola tugged me over to a wall where there was a C-shaped crack in the stone. *Come here, now, Claire-Bear,* she said, imitating Dad and pretending to snap a photo. *Look at the*

*perspective the artist used to craft the intricate design. Do you see
the C-shape of this piece of work? What do you think that might
be a symbol of?* We laughed and laughed.

How much time do we have? Lola finally asked me.

Like, twenty minutes.

Hide-and-seek? she asked sneakily.

Mom and Dad will kill us, I said. *We're supposed to stay
together.*

She grinned at me, looked around, and shrugged. *I'll hide
first,* she announced, and before I could say anything, she was
gone.

I turned in a circle, searching the crowd for Lola's face. No
one paid me any attention. They just walked around me as if I
were a rock.

I pushed through the tourists and the Chinese worshippers
and made my way over to a wall where there were fewer people,
so I could at least walk faster. I looked at my watch. I had fifteen
minutes to find Lola.

I ran from one end of the temple to the other. A guard in a
red shirt tapped me on the shoulder and sternly shook his finger
at me. *No to run,* he said. I ignored him, even though what he'd
said would normally make me smile. I went over to where Mom
and Dad had been looking at a small statue, but they weren't
there anymore. I sprinted to the giant Buddha—maybe Lola was
hiding somewhere around it. But I only saw a group of tourists
taking pictures as a different guard held up a sign warning them
not to use a flash.

I made my way toward the front doors, but Lola was nowhere to be found. My heart was racing and I was trying not to cry. I knew she was just playing, but I was so mad I hated her in that moment. What a *stupid* idea. She never even asked me if I wanted to play, and I *didn't*, and she was gone.

I ran to the back of the temple, hoping I'd see Mom and Dad, but also hoping I wouldn't, so I could at least find Lola first. I checked my watch. Less than ten minutes left. Through the open doorways, people wandered around a balcony over-looking the hills. I was scared to step out of the temple—Mom had said to stay inside—but I had to see if Lola was hiding on the balcony. Over by the edge there was a beggar sitting on a mat, selling sticks of incense. A family of tourists was getting their picture taken with the mountains in the background. The beggar was asking them for money and they were ignoring him. I leaned over the railing and looked down at the garden below.

And that's when I saw Lola.

She was sitting on a stone bench next to one of the ponds, completely out in the open. I felt like punching her for running away from me. Or shoving her right into the pond. What kind of hiding place was *that*, anyway? If Lola was going to make me run all over the stupid temple frantically searching for her, trying not to cry, she could have at least found someplace awesome to hide.

Then I realized she wasn't hiding—she was watching. There was a Chinese family across the pond from her: a mom and a dad and a baby girl. The little girl had a ponytail on the top of her head—a sprout of hair sticking straight up. It reminded me of Lola's hair in our first picture of her. The baby was squatting by the pond, reaching for fish in the water, as her mom held the back of her jacket so she wouldn't fall in. The father was taking pictures of them. Then the dad handed his camera to another tourist so he could join his wife and baby in a photo. The baby reached out for her father, and he took her in his arms and kissed her on the cheek. He and his wife stood side by side, each smiling down at their daughter as the tourist snapped their picture.

Lola was watching it all, and I didn't feel mad at her anymore. Someone came up right behind me and I turned around to find Dad. He and Mom must have seen me standing there, peering down at Lola. The Chinese family put their baby into a stroller and left before Mom, Dad, and I joined Lola in the garden. When we sat down on the bench with her, she remained as still as a stone. Mom and Dad never asked us why we weren't together, and they never yelled at us for not meeting them at the Buddha statue inside. We just sat there together, not saying anything, watching the sun get lower and lower in the hazy sky over the hills.

Chapter 21

Yuming

I'M STILL CLUTCHING the bills from the kind couple, and it dawns on me that it doesn't seem wise to be standing here on this crowded wall, holding so much money in my hand. Once I find the others—and I *will* find them—will Kai insist that we share it? Surely I can't just hide it from him. Where would I be without him? Inside the factory—that's where.

I crouch at the side of the Wall, take off my damp right shoe, and tuck the money inside. Then I watch the backs of the kind couple as they disappear into the crowd.

I think, once again, of Mama's back as she walked away. Why didn't I run after her? Or did I conjure that memory?

And Bolin—why didn't I search for him *before* Wai Gong and Wai Po died?

I start to jog again. I search each face that I pass. I have let too many people leave me. I won't let it happen again.

I approach the stone archway near the ticket stand where visitors enter and exit the Wall, and pass the giant rock with BADALING painted on it in red. The road beyond the ticket stand has become crowded with tourists. Most are walking toward me, past the small souvenir stands, the restaurants, and an American coffee shop.

Yesterday, as the bus pulled into the parking lot, Kai told us that the coffee shop was known among the beggars as the best place for handouts, so I glance around one more time, and jog over to its glass doorway. Maybe that's where he, Li, and Jing went. I need to find Jing. I need to tell her that I do not want her to leave me.

Inside, it is crowded and unfamiliar. The scent of brewing coffee is overwhelming. Wai Gong used to scoff at Chinese coffee drinkers. *Coffee?* he would exclaim in disbelief. *What happened to tea?* My eyes focus on a glass case filled with unusual-looking pastries and sandwiches. I am reminded of my biology teacher saying, *In the wild, the drive for food is more powerful than anything else.* I feel as if I am in the wild now.

I tear my eyes from the food, though, and spin around. Tables are filled with tourists drinking from steaming white paper cups. Their breakfast leftovers clutter the tables, torturing my empty stomach. Painted on the back wall is a green-and-brown map of the world, and I think of Bolin's map—so vast, and never offering any hint to his whereabouts. I search the

· 167 ·

faces all around me, looking for Jing, Kai, and Li, and, even though I know it is senseless, for Bolin.

A new tour group enters, and I gasp. My legs freeze. Among the crowd, his yellow Windbreaker casting a hideous, sickly glow onto his face, is Mr. Zhang.

Energy bolts through me. I back up, dipping behind the customers who surround me, until I am near the hallway leading to the bathrooms. I don't remove my eyes from his face even for a second—not even to blink. His eyes are hard. They're filled with fury, but his body is relaxed, as if he's trying to fit in as just another Chinese tourist getting coffee before visiting the Great Wall. He checks the long line at his left. His gaze is thorough and searching—just like mine. It is the look of someone who will not fail, who will find what he is looking for, who will find *us*.

His eyes are those of an animal—a predator. I, too, am an animal as I watch him. But I will not be his prey. I anticipate the way his gaze will shift and, when his eyes begin to wander away from the line of customers, I duck into the empty corridor. I feel nauseous as I walk quickly—with silent steps—toward the bathroom. I open the wooden door marked WOMEN and pull it closed it behind me.

The room swims before me. It is the most beautiful restroom I have ever seen.

Porcelain sinks hang from the wall, which is covered in shining, tiny, multicolored tiles. Each toilet is tucked into its own clean stall. The tiled floor underfoot gleams. On the back wall, small windows near the ceiling open to what I assume is an alleyway behind the coffee shop. My eyes rest on them.

I stand in the corner, my heart pounding, next to the door and near a silver paper-towel dispenser. A mother and her two daughters are washing their hands, talking in a language I don't know. Two of the four stalls are occupied, and I contemplate hiding inside one of the others, perched atop the fancy Western toilet so my feet aren't visible. Would Mr. Zhang have the audacity to walk into the women's bathroom? In my mind I can see his smooth face, his oily hair, his bone-white hands and dirty fingernails. Again, I remember the feel of his fist slamming into my head. . . .

The sisters and their mother take paper towels, wipe their hands, and reach for the door handle. I back into one of the stalls.

"Pardon me," I hear, as the bathroom door swings shut. I'm sure the voice is Mr. Zhang's, but I rush out of the stall and press my ear against the door, just to make sure. The *chug, chug, chugging* of my pulse threatens to choke me. "I'm looking for two young girls—my nieces. Long hair, white shirts, blue pants."

The mother of the two girls responds in her own language.

"Two girls!" Zhang says again, louder this time, as if that will help them comprehend his Chinese. I imagine his eyes narrowing to slits. I can see him holding up two fingers.

The mother responds quickly and harshly in words I do not know.

"You are worthless!" I hear Zhang yell, and I imagine they're walking away from him quickly. Perhaps they can sense that he is a predator.

I wonder how long he will stand there by the closed bathroom door, an animal sniffing out its prey.

A stall opens, and a Chinese lady emerges to wash her hands. Mr. Zhang will ask her about us next. I walk briskly back to the stall, where I'll have to continue hiding. I keep my eyes on the bathroom doorway in the mirror. As I am about to duck back into the stall, another one opens. Jing walks out.

My heart leaps with joy, and floods with anger. Her face is pale. Before I can say anything, she whispers, "What is wrong?" Then I realize why she looks frightened: She is reacting to how *I* look. I reach for her hand and try to act calm.

"Come," I say. "Let's get a towel."

She studies my face, trying to figure me out, as I drag her back to the corner of the washroom behind the door. The Chinese woman has dried her hands. She glances at us while she pulls the door open and walks out. I grip Jing's arm to hold her back and put a finger to my lips.

"Pardon me," Mr. Zhang says. Jing freezes. "Did you see two girls in the washroom?"

I hold my breath, awaiting the woman's response. She is silent at first. "Two girls?" she finally asks.

"Yes. *Two girls.*"

I stare at Jing. Her wide eyes search the bathroom. They stop and I follow her gaze to the high square windows on the back wall. But it's useless. Mr. Zhang will burst through this doorway before we could even reach them. He'll grab us and drag us—

"No," the woman replies. "I did not see them."

I am so overcome with relief my knees almost give way, but I catch myself.

"Well, are you sure or not?" Mr. Zhang snaps, as though he doesn't believe her.

We are not safe yet. Jing's jaw is clenched. Her hands are shaking. I push my ear to the door, but I can't hear anything outside. Before anyone else can come in, I pull her to the opposite wall.

"It was stupid to come here," I hiss, anger overcoming my relief at finding Jing. "He knew just where to find us. Kai *said* this coffeehouse was the best place to beg."

"Kai . . ." Jing replies weakly. "He stole a backpack from a Japanese tourist. It was filled with food! He and Li are eating in the alley behind this building. I was just on my way to go back and get you. We need to hurry. Mr. Zhang might check back there."

It's almost too much information to take in. And I still don't know why they all left me this morning. But I don't have time to ask her about that now. "He's probably out there in the coffee shop," I whisper. "It would be foolish to leave so soon."

Jing points up to the windows and I nod. Together, we put a tall garbage can directly below the windows. "Quick," I say. Jing climbs on top of the lid first as I hold the narrow metal bin steady. She pushes a screen out of one of the windows. I hear it clatter to the ground outside before she hoists herself up and quickly disappears through the frame.

Hoping no one else will come in to use the restroom, I awkwardly clamber onto the garbage can and scramble for the window. Behind me, the door creaks open as I swing one leg over the window ledge and pivot to face the inside of the bathroom. Humid wind lifts my shirt in back. A lady walks in and calls out, "Hey!" when she sees me. Behind her, squinting into the room, is Mr. Zhang.

Before I have time to think, I am already dropping to the ground—too fast and with no control. I can smell car exhaust, like the exhaust of Mr. Zhang's bus. I can hear the sewing machines again already.

I land painfully on gray dirt. Jing, Kai, and Li are waiting for me. "He saw me!" I yell as I get to my feet. "We have to get away from here!" I start racing toward the street that leads to the parking lot.

The others follow and Jing grabs for my hand. "We cannot get separated!" she yells, and my heart threatens to burst. I squeeze her thin, cold hand. The crowds are thick. Mr. Zhang will be rounding the side of the coffee shop at any moment to look for us behind it. I push my way through a clump of foreigners. We duck between two souvenir stands and jump down from a low cement wall into the parking lot. I glance over my shoulder for a second. Li is holding Jing's other hand, and Kai is close behind.

"Nice escape," Kai says to me, panting, when we gather behind a tour bus. I study him as though I'm seeing the real him for the first time. Leaving me beneath the Great Wall, asleep, with that man and his dog—that was foolish. I don't blame Li—he's too young. I should blame Kai and Jing equally, but, for some reason, I only blame Kai. *She'll be fine,* I imagine him saying to Jing. *Let her sleep. I'll teach you to pickpocket. We can always come back for her later.* Kai feels like a risk I can't afford.

Behind us is another bus—a city bus. I pull the others toward it. "We need to jump on just as it's leaving," Kai whispers, tugging me back by my shirt.

I picture Mr. Zhang popping out from the other side of the tour bus. I can see the pale-pink factory. I can feel the hunger, the boredom, and the loneliness as I attach purse handles for hours on end for the rest of my life. "No," I say. "Follow me. I have money."

I dash quickly onto the bus, kick off my filthy shoe, pull out the sweaty wad of bills, and hand them to the driver. "Four, please," I say, shaking. I feel Kai's eyes on me.

The driver looks me over, surprised, but takes the money and hands me some change. I don't stop to count it. Jing, Kai, and Li climb the steps behind me. We head for the back of the bus and duck into the last two rows of seats.

Kai sits beside me, sweat rolling down his face, and peers at me suspiciously. "Where'd you—?"

"Duck down!" Jing hisses. "Just in case."

Exhaust chokes me as the bus idles; I try to will it to move. I lean my forehead against the seat in front of me and squeeze my eyes shut. It's early in the day, and I'm already so tired. Tired of this life "on the streets." There are too many risks; too much is dependent on everybody else. I can't think any more about the *what-ifs*. If Mr. Zhang saw us board the bus, we're done for—that's all I need to know.

I pray to Wai Po's and Wai Gong's spirits. *Please, get us out of here safely.*

The bus lurches into gear and begins to rumble forward. I sit up, the back of my head on the window. In front of me, a bored-looking teenage boy sits beside his father.

"Pardon me," I say to him softly. "Can you tell me where this bus is headed?"

He looks at me as if I'm an idiot. "Didn't you see the big sign in the window? Sunma," he says, putting his headphones over his ears.

"The kite festival is this weekend," the boy's father adds, smiling at me kindly despite my ragged appearance.

"Yes," Kai whispers to himself with great relief, leaning back. I turn to him. "What?"

"Sunma is far from here. Way north of the city."

"North of the city . . . . Isn't that where the factory is?" I whisper.

"It's not far from the factory, yes, but still it is a good place for us. Dan Temple is there. Lots of tourists! And," he says, lowering his voice even more, his eyes gleaming, "the kite festival will be perfect for pickpocketing lessons."

The bus slowly makes its way through the crowded parking lot, leaving the Great Wall behind. But it's taking me *farther* from Shanghai—farther from where I need to be. And I don't want to be a pickpocket. I sift through the dirty bills the driver handed back to me. After buying the four bus tickets, I have forty yuan left, which surely won't be enough for a ticket anywhere.

"Where did you get all that—?" Kai begins again, but I sit forward, bombarded by a thought.

"Mr. Zhang—" I interrupt. "If he saw us get onto the bus, he'll follow us."

"What?" Kai asks.

"The sign," I go on. "There's a sign on the bus that says Sunma!"

"Oh, that," Kai goes on, leaning back and closing his eyes. "Well, that would be unlikely."

Unlikely, I think, looking desperately at Jing in the seat behind mine. Li is leaning against her, falling asleep, oblivious to it all. Unlikely, but possible.

"Not worth the risk," Jing whispers, careful not to wake Li, her eyes locked on mine. "We can't stay there long."

Chapter 22

July 8th
Sunma, Hebei Province, China

Clara

I CAN'T GET the memory out of my mind. I remember how furious I was with Lola for making me search all over that crowded temple, thinking the entire time, What if she's gone? Now I feel furious all over again.

"What time is it?" I ask Mom as we walk down the steep stone staircase.

She looks at her watch. "Just about noon."

I could be so close to Yuming's factory right now, and I'm getting desperate. We only have a few more hours here, and I need to make something *happen*. I picture myself opening an ordinary-looking door in a huge pink factory and finding a room full of thin, overworked children inside. I picture Yuming looking up from her sewing machine, her eyes meeting mine. I need to get some more information about this area.

Across the narrow street is the huge park. A few food and souvenir stands are clustered together near the entrance, and I watch a vendor hand ice cream bars to a woman and a little boy. Next to that stand, an old man is selling kites. Spools of string hang from an awning above him and the walls of his stand are cluttered with bright kites shaped like dragons, panda bears, and birds. I glance around. *Think, Clara, think!* Lola yells in my ear. Who here could help me?

"We should eat ice cream for lunch," Mom announces.

"Brilliant idea," Dad agrees.

We make our way down the temple stairs. At the stand, I study the flavors in the refrigerated box, still wracking my brain for a way—*some* way—to find out about the factory. I never liked the Chinese flavors as much as Lola did, but I'm hungry, so I pull out a bar with a drawing of lychee nuts on it because it was Lola's favorite. We show it to the vendor before I unwrap it, and I wander away from Mom and Dad, over to the kite stand. The old man is sitting on a crate, gluing a wooden rod to the dragon kite he's working on.

Two years ago, there was a huge kite festival in Shanghai, and we spent an entire morning there. It was sunny and clear, and the bright-blue sky looked amazing with millions of kites flying against it. We stayed until the smog blew back in.

I bend down to carefully touch a red dragon kite on a blanket on the ground. It reminds me of Lola's kite from last time, except hers was pink. The vendor smiles at me as a girl about my age skips over and joins him. She asks him something in Chinese and then turns to me. "Have you come for kite festival?"

Ask her! Lola would say. I glance over at Mom and Dad. They're sifting through some postcards on a rack as they eat their ice cream. "Oh, no," I say quickly. "I didn't know there was one. We just came to see Dan Temple."

"Dan Si is very nice. The kite festival is today and tomorrow. Begins at six o'clock tonight."

I nod. That sounds cool, but I need to find out about the pink factory. "Um, do you know this area well?" I ask the girl quietly. Out of the corner of my eye, I see Mom and Dad glance my way.

"I have lived here my whole life," she says, lowering her voice, too, and eyeing me curiously.

"Have you ever seen a pink factory in this area?" I whisper.

"A pink factory?" she repeats in a whisper. "Let me ask my uncle."

I nod. I barely have *any* time to get this done—to get to Yuming. I need to save her, and suddenly I feel like I might cry.

Mom and Dad start to walk toward me. The girl is asking the old man something quietly in Chinese, and my heart starts thumping. This girl and old man might just have all the information I need, but if they say something about the factory in front of Mom and Dad, my entire plan will be ruined; the entire *trip* will be ruined.

I feel dizzy. The old man responds, glancing at me and gesturing with his paint-splattered hands. The girl turns back to me and gives me a secretive little nod before saying to Mom and Dad, "We have wonderful kite festival here. Today and tomorrow. Will you stay for it?" My breathing steadies.

"There's a kite festival here?" Mom asks.

"Yes," the girl says. "A big festival, which begins in a few hours. Here, in this park. It begins again at sunrise tomorrow. Very famous kite festival. Many people are setting up for it already!" She points behind her, where several stands are being erected.

"Oh, we didn't know," Mom says, excitedly. "We should stay through dinner!"

"Yeah, let's stay," I add quickly, glancing at the girl.

"Yes," she chimes in, smiling directly at me. "Stay."

"Al, let's do it!" Mom goes on. "Remember how Lola loved the kites in Shanghai?" I watch the girl's face as she looks from Mom to Dad.

Dad nods. "Yeah," he says wistfully, "I remember. I guess we could stay through dinner. We were going to try that restaurant near our hotel, though. . . ."

"Oh, who cares about that?" Mom says before I can even open my mouth. "Let's stay. Come on, it will be an adventure!"

"Would you like to buy a kite?" the girl asks. "My uncle makes each kite by hand. Very strong. Will not break." Lola's first dragon kite had broken last time. She was so upset that Mom and Dad had bought her another.

"Let's buy one!" I say to Mom and Dad.

"And," the girl goes on, "you will have the rest of the afternoon to enjoy Sunma. This is a very historic city with special tourist attractions. For example, we have a wonderful gondola that will take you high into the hills and allow you views of the area." She looks at me intently. "From up high, you are able to see *all you need to see* of Beijing and Hebei Province, from a section of the Great Wall of China just south of here, to the many factories to our northwest."

My heart leaps. "That sounds beautiful," I say to Mom and Dad quickly, still looking at the girl. She is smiling politely at us.

"It does," Mom agrees. "And it's a pretty clear day—we'll be able to see a lot." Bands of white clouds hang like streamers across the rare light-blue sky.

"Can we do it, Dad?" I ask. "It will be so cool to see everything." My pulse is racing. This could be it! "Where do we get the gondola?" I ask the girl.

She points to her right. "Two blocks that way, you will see the base of it. Look up that way into the hills. Do you see the cable?"

I squint at the thick green trees in the foothills and nod. "There it is," I say to Mom and Dad, pointing to the silver wire that runs from post to post up the mountainside.

"The entire ride up and down is one hour, and very scenic," the girl goes on. "You'll be able to see *everything*." She stresses the word, and I grin at her. I want to hug her.

"Let's go!" I say to Mom and Dad.

"It sounds nice," Mom says to the girl. "Thank you for the suggestion."

"Have a good day," Dad adds, starting to walk away.

"Would you like a kite for the festival?" the girl calls after us.

"Right," I say, thinking I should pay her back for helping me. "How about a dragon one? In honor of Lola?"

"I don't know," Mom says. "Those are so big. . . . Maybe when we return from the ride?"

"I would not wait," says the girl. "It gets very crowded. My uncle makes the best kites; they will be gone."

"All right, sure," Dad says, unzipping his fanny pack.

The old man takes Dad's money and lifts a blue-and-gold dragon kite off the wall of the stand. "The dragon is a symbol of luck," the girl says, looking me in the eye.

Lola would have loved her. "Thank you," I tell her. She nods again, still smiling, and we walk toward the gondola ride.

The dragon kite feels sturdy. It's hard to carry because it's heavy and huge. I'm so excited that I want to let out the string and run with it now. I can picture it sailing up into the humid breeze, bright against the sky.

There's only a small crowd at the gondola booth. Dad buys three tickets and we get into line to board. I hold tight to my dragon and try to relax. The girl's uncle was a really old man; it's possible he was wrong about whatever he told her. And what if she was just trying to make a sale? Even if she was really trying to help, I may see factories, but not a *pink* factory. This isn't a sure thing, I tell myself as we inch forward.

We're next to board, and the gondola slows down in front of us. I can't help feeling optimistic as a young man opens the door for us. Dad hands him our tickets and we step inside. I rest my kite against one of the benches and we sit down. Another couple that looks American climbs in, too, and the attendant outside slides the door shut and locks it.

Mom and Dad introduce themselves to the couple, who tell us they are from Toronto. Our car speeds up, emerges from the station, and begins climbing the foothills. My stomach drops a little as the ground gets farther away. The surrounding area is still hidden from view by the tall trees on the mountainside, and I can't wait to get up and over them, so I can see what the girl said I would to see. I'm thankful when Mom and Dad strike up a conversation with the other couple so I can look out the window in peace.

My heart thuds harder and harder as we rise. Soon, the entire landscape bursts into sight. I tell myself to relax, and I focus on breathing evenly. Freaking out isn't going to help me—I know that. But I need to find Yuming's factory, and I look from one window of the gondola to the other. I can see the park now on one side; a few kites are flying above the grass. There's a fountain at the far side, and I think of Lola and Yuming's fountain in Shanghai. I get up on my knees and look behind us, beyond Sunma. Way off in the distance, tall buildings stretch into the sky: Beijing.

"Beautiful day for this," the Canadian woman is saying. "We were here two years ago for three weeks, and we never once saw blue sky."

"We're very lucky," Dad agrees, and they continue to chat.

To my left, Sunma stretches into the mountainside. Its houses and buildings become smaller and smaller as we climb, until they're just a mass of white squares and rectangles along-side a winding river.

"Is that north?" I interrupt, pointing left.

"What, honey?" Mom asks, smiling over at me.

"I'm just wondering—which way is north? And which is south?" I add quickly. "I just want to know where I'm looking."

"I believe that's north," the Canadian woman tells me kindly, pointing out the window to her right. I get up and move to the empty seat across from her.

"Thanks," I say, pressing my nose to the smudged glass.

I see a valley with a tiny village at the bottom of it. Beyond it, spread apart along the base of the jagged mountains, are several buildings with smokestacks. Those must be factories!

I gasp quietly and look over the scene that is laid out in front of me like a drawing in a picture book. My heart pounding, I count five factories in the foothills. Their smokestacks spew white billows onto the pale-blue background. I touch Yuming's photograph in one pocket, and Lola's ashes in the other. Sunlight reflects off of the buildings scattered in the distance, but it's not hard to tell—it's not hard *at all* to tell—that one of the factories is pink.

Chapter 23

July 8th
Sunma, Hebei Province, China

Yuming

"CAN'T STAY LONG?" Kai asks, sitting on his knees and looking back at Jing. "That would be a mistake." His anger only barely masks his anxiety. I look from him to Jing to Li, who is sleeping soundly now, his hands twitching in his lap.

"So then," I say, "what do you suggest?"

"For now, it's best to eat and rest." Kai brusquely unzips the backpack that he stole, filled with snack food. "We have a few hours on this bus—two, maybe three. Then, with the kite festival crowds, we can stay hidden and busy in Sunma." His smile appears forced. "I began Jing's lessons while you slept this morning. Now it's time for me to start teaching *you* the ways of the streets."

I feel relief at hearing that Kai is committed to staying with me, but I don't *want* to learn the ways of the streets.

I squeeze my eyes shut. I recall a winter day years ago. Bolin and I had an argument on the way to school. I don't even remember what it was about, but he walked quickly down the narrow road to the schoolhouse ahead of me, his back growing smaller and smaller with every step. I slowed down, watching as he sped up and, ultimately, disappeared from sight.

Deep down I know that, no matter where I go, no matter how hard I search, I will never be able to catch up with him. My best chance of seeing him again will be to get back to Yemo Village, where he will surely come to visit *someday.* . . .

My mind swimming, I glance toward Jing and Li again. Li's cheeks are rosy and his bony chest rises and falls deeply with every breath. It amazes me how he can sleep through anything. His innocence reminds me of myself—of how I used to be before Wai Po and Wai Gong died.

I force myself to focus—to evaluate my options and measure the risks. *I can do this, Wai Gong. Don't worry, Wai Po.*

"It is possible that Mr. Zhang saw us board and will follow this bus to Sunma. And even if that's not the case, I don't want to be anywhere near that factory," I say to Kai and Jing. "I think we need to immediately leave Sunma when this bus lets us off."

Jing nods, as though she's thinking. Kai doesn't respond.

"How much money do you have left?" Jing whispers, trying not to wake Li. "And how did you get that, anyway?"

"A man and woman—they just handed it to me," I say. "Only forty yuan left."

"Sunma will be filled to the brim with rich tourists," Kai says. "I'm not passing up an opportunity to make great money."

"*Make* money?" I ask, angry now, thinking of Wai Gong and the long hours he'd spend hunched in the rice fields. Once, after we drove into town to exchange a portion of the crop for money, Wai Gong was pickpocketed. It was only after we returned home that he realized his wallet was missing. Then he remembered a young man who had stumbled into him near the government truck. The man had grasped Wai Gong for support and Wai Gong had helped him steady himself. And just like that, all of our rice money had vanished.

"Yes, good girl—*make* money," Kai continues.

"Pickpocketing isn't making money," I whisper, furious. "It's *stealing* money."

"How else are we supposed to survive?" Kai asks me bluntly.

I search my brain for an answer, because there must be a better way. "We could go to a different city and ask a police officer there for help. You could come south—with me—to Shanghai. The police there won't be on Mr. Zhang's side."

"And how will we get across the country with only forty yuan?" Kai sighs in exasperation.

"You're going to Shanghai?" Jing asks, leaning forward suddenly. I try to read the expression on her face.

"It's where *Princess* is from," Kai tells her, glaring at me. "And anyway, what will become of me and Li if we go to a police officer in *any* city? Li would be taken to an orphanage, that's what. That is not the life for us," he whispers emphatically. It's true, what he says; I can't picture the two of them separated, Li in an orphanage, attending school every day and sleeping in a row of neat cots every night while Kai prowls the streets on his own.

"This life," he goes on, "this life on the streets, it's what I know. I like it. I belong on the streets. No, I'm staying here. A few days in Sunma, and then back to Beijing—back to the streets we know."

"That's so close to Mr. Zhang, though," Jing says, looking from me to Kai.

"And close to Mama," Li mumbles, his little sleepy face sweaty, his cheeks red with heat.

Kai glares in Li's direction.

I open my mouth to ask Kai about his mother, but then shut it.

"Kai," Jing says. She looks down at her fingers. "I don't think I can stay in Sunma. It's too close to the factory." She pauses, her eyes locked on mine, before looking back at Kai. "I'd never feel safe."

"Come with me, then," I say, getting up on my knees. Nervous about her response, I look down at the cracked plastic of the bus seat. "I don't want . . ." I steal a glance at her. "I don't want us to be separated."

Jing doesn't respond, and I turn to face the window. We're rumbling through a small village. Three old men stand on the roadside, watching our bus pass; a grandmother and young girl on a motorcycle race by; the door to a restaurant closes behind a customer. I watch the blur of so many lives as the bus speeds forward.

"Shanghai is by the sea, no?" Jing finally asks me.

I look back at her. "Yes," I tell her. "Right by the sea."

"Is it beautiful where you come from?"

I nod, thinking of *my* golden sea, three hours inland: the sprawling rice fields. It was a strong crop the summer that Bolin left, and the fields radiated yellow. When we returned from dropping him off in Shanghai, I sat on the edge of the field, where the swaying crop faded into fog-covered mountains. Fog to more fog, mountains to endless mountains, all under the white sky that stretched into forever. I remember longing for my sibling.

"Yes," Jing says, her eyes locked on mine. "I'd like that."

Kai huffs dismissively and sinks lower in his seat.

I only nod, because I have a lump in my throat. I think yet again of how I excluded Jing from our initial escape plan because I thought it would be risky to include her. If it weren't for her solitary measurement of risks and options, she would not be with me now. I cannot imagine the past days without her, and this thought frightens me—how each of our decisions leads to the next, and how everything is dependent upon whatever came before.

Li coughs and sits up, asleep and awake all at once. "You all right, Li?" Jing asks, looking away from my eyes and rubbing his back. He nods and coughs some more, leaning on Jing again. She lowers her window so the breeze can wash over his sweaty face. I sit back, next to Kai, and watch Hebei Province slide by through the dirty bus window, thinking, all the time, of Shanghai, of Yemo Village, of being home with Jing. And, someday, Bolin. The thought makes me want to cry tears of happiness.

We pass stretches of trees and small villages, a family of five all crammed onto a tractor, old men with wheelbarrows on the side of the road. I am almost home, I think. Hungrily, we gobble the food from the backpack. Eventually, the green hills around us fall away, exposing a sprawling town ahead. In the center, high above the buildings, stands a large red temple. The sky overhead is a rare light blue.

"Dan Temple," Kai whispers, as if to himself. A sign on the roadside reads WELCOME TO SUNMA.

I touch my pants pocket. I don't know the cost of train tickets to Shanghai, but surely it is infinitely more than the forty yuan I'm carrying. Perhaps it is almost enough for two tickets? *Almost enough is not enough,* I imagine Wai Po saying, but I can't think of her now—her soft skin, her soft white hair, her soft lullabies. I have to focus on one thing: We need more money.

Chapter 24

Clara

I PRESS MY forehead against the glass so Mom and Dad won't be able to see the tears that are trying to jump out of my eyes. They're still chatting away with the other couple, talking about hotel rates in Sunma, the kite festival, and the Canadians' Siberian husky back home. They're not paying any attention to me. And that's fine.

Focus, Lola would tell me. *Map it out—hurry! How would you get there from the base of the gondola?* I look out the back window, down at the rolling hills, Sunma, and the tree-covered mountains. I can see the roof of the temple with its layers of curving red tile. There are the ponds where Lola watched the Chinese baby reaching for the koi fish. Beyond Sunma is the tiny, run-down-looking village at the bottom of the valley, and up above it, just before the mountain juts straight up into the sky, is a pink factory. Yuming's factory. Three of the four smokestacks spew exhaust into the sky. I whisper silent messages and try to force them through the air. *I'm coming for you, Yuming! I'm coming.*

Being so close makes me feel frantic, just like I did right after Lola died. Once I found Yuming's picture and note, I started seeing Lola everywhere, and that had made the anxious feeling disappear. Now, knowing Yuming is so close, but not being able to do anything for her yet . . . It makes my whole body want to explode.

I imagine Lola standing next to me inside the cable car. I see her smile at me in a mischievous kind of way before she opens the sliding window. Her ghostlike image climbs out and up, onto the top of the car. I cringe and my stomach feels suddenly like it's floating through air that's too thin. *This is awesome!* Lola calls down to me. *I'm gonna go check out the factory.*

I feel like yelling to Lola, even though I *know* she's not really here.

Come with me! Lola says, peeking her head back into the window from above, her hair draping down like a black, silky curtain. I look down, all the way to the ground, where doll-size people are hiking on a trail.

All right, scaredy-cat! I'm going, then!

Lola leaps off the top of the cable car—she's flying, her arms outstretched, her hair blowing out behind her. She turns her head back to me, and smiles as she soars. I watch her get smaller and smaller as she gets closer and closer to the pink factory. She lands right on top of it, just a tiny speck now. I picture her, transparent, ghostly, slipping through a doorway and into Yuming's sewing room. I see her sitting down next to the Chinese girl who has been stuck in a factory prison for who knows how long. The two girls are so similar in my mind—they're both bold and brave. They're so similar that they're almost the same person.

I have a wild urge to climb out the window after the ghost of my sister—the ghost that I *know* isn't real. I feel like I'm going crazy.

I squeeze my eyes shut and force myself to breathe. I switch seats so I'm next to Mom, and she puts her arm around me. "Beautiful views, huh?" she says softly, and I know that what she's really thinking is *Lola would have loved this*. "You okay, honey?"

I nod and force myself to smile. "Just tired," I say, leaning my head back against the hard plastic seat and closing my eyes. "Jet lag."

Unlike Lola's ghost, I can't skydive, and I can't fly. I need a real-life plan. That's what Lola would say if she were still here. *You need a plan.*

☆

Back on the ground, I walk ahead of Mom and Dad, who are still talking to their new friends. Dad is carrying my dragon kite. I still feel like I'm floating in the cable car as I lead the way back toward the park. Up ahead, colorful kites dot the light-blue, cloud-laced sky.

"I didn't realize how well-known this festival is," Dad says to me, handing me my kite once we reach the park. He straightens out the gold ribbons on the dragon. "Marcy and Mason told us they've been planning their trip here for months."

"Yeah, cool," I tell him absently, still thinking. Mom, Marcy, and Mason join us.

"What a great kite," Marcy says.

"Thanks," I say. "That man over there made it." I point to where he's still sitting, across the street from us. It does look like he has sold a lot of kites, like his niece had predicted. She is nowhere in sight.

I keep picturing Lola inside of Yuming's factory. I need to get to Yuming. "So, there's more going on tomorrow?" I ask Marcy.

"Oh, yes! I was telling your mom and dad—tomorrow morning there's a big kite ceremony with a twenty-meter-long dragon kite! Should be spectacular!"

I turn to my parents. "We should stay for that," I say. I wish Lola were here to help me convince them. Instead, she is sitting side by side with Yuming in front of a sewing machine. "We should stay in Sunma tonight."

"Oh, honey, I'd love that," Mom says. "But all our stuff is back at the hotel, and, anyway, I'm sure there aren't any rooms available here. Hotels will have been booked far in advance."

"True," Mason pipes in. "Unless you want to stay in the room next to us with no bathroom," he jokes.

"What do you mean?" I ask quickly, picturing Yuming and Lola looking up from the sewing machine.

"Oh, apparently, the room that joins up with ours doesn't have a working bathroom," Mason says. "The only reason we know this is because the Korean couple that had booked it left in a huff."

"That's a shame," Mom says.

"The manager kept pointing to a washroom at the end of the hall, but they wanted nothing to do with that," Marcy goes on. "I don't blame them. They probably reserved the room ages ago."

I look at Mom and Dad. "Do you think that room is still available?" I ask Marcy.

"I'd imagine so," she says. "I don't know who would want to stay in a room with no bathroom."

"I bet you could get that room very cheaply!" Mason chimes in.

"Yeah, can we?" I plead. I'm so close now. I have to get to Yuming; I *have* to save her.

"It would be fun," Dad says. "But, like Mom said before, we don't have any of our stuff. And we've already paid for the room in Beijing."

"And no bathroom?" Mom asks.

"But . . . but Lola would have loved this," I stammer. "She loved the kite festival in Shanghai, and the giant dragon kite— remember how they had something like that at the other one? Remember how much she loved it?"

"I remember, honey," Mom says. "But it just doesn't make

any sense. We were going to have dinner at that restaurant near the hotel. And then, tomorrow we were going to do the Beijing museums. . . ."

But I need more time to save Yuming! I want to scream. I'm sure my face is turning red, and I'm trying not to cry. The adults are looking at me curiously.

Mom glances at Marcy and Mason. She looks tired, and like she doesn't feel like explaining everything that's happened to us in the past few months. "Honey," she repeats sadly, "it just doesn't make sense. I'm sorry."

"The ashes," I say suddenly. "Lola's ashes. I might want to do something with them here. Tomorrow." The lies come easily. "Lola loved the dragon at the kite festival, and I think I want to do something with her ashes." Marcy and Mason are staring at me, and Mom and Dad look like they're going to cry now, too. "But tomorrow morning," I say again. "Not yet."

Mom nods slowly. She turns to Marcy and Mason. "I'm so sorry," she says. Dad nods at her, like he's relieved, and Mom turns back to me. "Okay, sweetie. Let's go see if that room with no bathroom is still available."

I realize I've been holding my breath, and I exhale. Marcy and Mason look confused, but they lead us through the park, under strings and soaring kites, to an old building that says SUNMA VILLAGE HOTEL over the doorway.

"It's very historic," Marcy says awkwardly, like she's trying to make conversation.

"Gorgeous," Mom adds absently, studying me.

"Can I meet you out here?" I ask, pointing to the hotel steps.

Mom and Dad look at each other. "Sure," Dad says. "We'll be right out. You know where we are if you need us."

I nod and sit down on the cool stone step, my blue dragon kite in my lap.

Chapter 25

July 8th
Sunma, Hebei Province, China

Yuming

KAI GRUNTS AS he lifts Li off the bus seat. There are many people ahead of us, still waiting to depart, but Kai stands, holding his brother, anyway. "So lazy," he mutters as Li rests his head on his brother's shoulder, but Kai's eyes look strangely nervous. "Yuming, you have forty yuan, right?"

"Yes." I look at Li again. He is very sweaty. I wonder what Kai is thinking—that the money won't be nearly enough for Jing and me to get to Shanghai? That half of it should go to him and Li? Twenty yuan is barely anything, but he would be correct. After all, without them, I'd still be sewing in the factory.

Kai nods, his eyes darting around the bus. In front of us, waiting in the aisle to depart, is the bored teenager, still listening to his music, and behind him, just in front of Kai, stands the boy's father. I swallow hard, watching Kai's shifting eyes. I watch them until they shift onto me.

I look down. "Yuming," Kai whispers, sliding back into the seat next to me, Li on his lap. "My hands are full."

"What does that have to do with anything?" I whisper quickly, even though I know.

His wallet, he mouths, rolling his eyes as though I'm some sort of idiot. He pulls me close. "Listen," he goes on, barely audible, "distraction is the key. He needs to think the pressure on his rear is from something else—something that will make him feel compassion for you and not question you."

I think again of the time Wai Gong lost all of his money and shake my head quickly. "No."

"I've got Li," Kai hisses. "How many hands do you think I have?"

"Give him to me," I whisper back. This is a lesson I do not need. Jing and I will be off soon to Shanghai, and this will no longer be my life.

But Kai shakes his head again, raising his eyebrows, as if he knows infinitely more than I do. "No," he says. "Li is peaceful now. I don't want to wake him. Do it."

Up ahead, near the bus door, the line begins to move and my heart leaps into my throat as I imagine Mr. Zhang waiting for us at the bottom of the steps. Kai jerks his head toward the front of the bus, as if I need a reminder that we don't have much time.

Jing and I *will* need more money to get home to Yemo Village. I stand up and squeeze past Kai and Li, feeling like I'm in someone else's body.

Hands shaking again, I stand in the aisle behind the man. The line creeps forward. Jing gets up behind me, and Kai gives me a soft kick to tell me to hurry up. I reach slowly into my pocket, where the photograph of my family *should* be, and I pull out one of the bills I have left. I drop it onto the dirty bus floor. It floats down and lands silently. "Excuse me?" I whisper.

The man doesn't respond.

"Pardon me?" I say, a bit louder.

He turns around. His eyes are sparkling black, and soft wrinkles surround them. I wonder, suddenly, if he was disappointed that his son listened to music the entire way to Sunma instead of talking to him. "Can I help you?" he asks.

I look to the floor again, flooded with shame. He follows my gaze. "Ah," he says, bending down to pick up the bill that landed near his freshly shined shoes. The wallet in his back pocket is only inches from me, but I cannot move; my hand is frozen. Kai kicks me again, but still, I stand there. I remember Wai Gong's face when he realized his wallet was gone and how he dreaded telling Wai Po.

The man stands up and hands me my money. I look at his feet and thank him as the line moves forward.

Kai swears quietly and shoves me aside with Li in his arms. I inch forward behind them, my face burning with shame—both because I'd thought of stealing from the man and because I wasn't able to. Now what? Jing and I need money if we're ever to get home.

Kai taps the kind man on his shoulder. "Pardon me?" he says. The man stops shuffling forward and turns around. "I apologize, but I believe my brother is ill." Kai's eyes are moist, and I think back to our escape from the cafeteria in the factory. I can't tell if he's scheming or serious. "Do you mind if I squeeze ahead of you?" he goes on. "I need to get him to a doctor."

"Of course," the man says, turning his body sideways. Kai edges past him slowly. Li's limp legs brush against the bus seat and then the man's pants. Kai swiftly pulls a black leather wallet from the man's back pocket—a wallet similar to the one Wai Gong had—and passes it to me.

It's thick; I'm sure it contains credit cards and bank cards and that taking it will ruin the man's vacation. I don't want to touch it, so I pass it quickly to Jing. She tucks it into the waistband of her pants, and I turn forward to watch Kai continue to make his way past the rest of the bus passengers and to the door.

The line begins to move faster and my heart *chug, chug, chugs* with fear that the man will notice his wallet is gone. I need to get off this bus and away from him, but Mr. Zhang . . . Is it possible that he could be waiting for us just outside? Kai and Li are almost there. I look from the kind man to the bus windows, searching for a yellow Windbreaker. My eyes dart back and forth as my mind jumps from the father to Mr. Zhang and then to Jing. I am grateful that this life will soon be a memory.

The man and his son climb down the steps. The father puts his hand on his son's shoulder, and they walk toward the street corner without acknowledging Kai and Li, who are waiting on the curb. I stand next to the driver, envisioning Mr. Zhang racing across the street toward us, whispering that he has a knife and if we scream, he will kill us.

My legs shake. The risk of being here, in this town, where Mr. Zhang could possibly come looking for us, feels like an unbearable mistake—an error of judgment. I can picture Wai Gong's disapproving eyes over the xiangqi board.

I turn to the bus driver as I run my hands over the money in my pocket. "Where are you headed to next?" I ask him.

"Yetu Village."

"Is that to the south?"

"Yes."

I nod. "How much per ticket?"

"Fifteen yuan."

I look back at Jing. She appears to be thinking intently as she follows our conversation, and she glances out the window to where Kai, still holding Li, is waiting, looking around nervously. I take the money out of my pocket. "We could do it," I whisper. "Get off, say a quick good-bye to the boys, give them—you know." I nod toward the elastic of her pants. "Then we could get back on—get away from here—away from Mr. Zhang. In Yetu Village, we will be safe, and we can figure out how to get to Shanghai."

"What's the holdup?" the driver asks impatiently. We are the last two people on the bus.

"What time do you depart?" I ask.

"As soon as you two get off," he says, glowering. "I drive up the street, fill with petrol, and come back here to pick up."

"What are you doing?" Kai calls to us over the sound of Li's coughing.

"All right," Jing says. "So get off. We'll figure it out." She peers deliberately through each window. "I don't see Mr. Zhang anywhere."

The bus driver sighs and looks at his watch.

I look through the windows, too, nod, and shove the money back in my pocket. Li hasn't stopped coughing. This doesn't seem safe, but we can't just leave without saying our good-byes to Kai and Li. And we can't keep all the money.

On the street, though, my heart races as the bus pulls away. The gravity of the mistake we may have just made floods me. I am once again an animal being hunted. Jing and I join Kai and Li, and we turn in slow circles, scouring the streets for the yellow Windbreaker, the sharp, evil eyes, the greedy hands until I am dizzy. "We need to get away from here," I say breathlessly. "This is the center of town—it's the first place Mr. Zhang would come looking."

"That's true," Jing says quickly. She's more nervous than I've ever seen her—perhaps because she's so close; so close to her freedom.

"We probably have ten minutes until the bus comes back," I say. "Let's move to—"

"What do you mean, 'until the bus comes back'?" Kai interrupts.

I glance at Jing. "We're going to go," she says, looking down. Li stirs and unpeels his head from Kai's shoulder. He straightens his back and coughs—a shallow and rumbling sound that reminds me of a crackling fire, and Wai Gong's cough.

"You're leaving *already*?" Kai asks, his face hard.

Jing nods.

"We need to get off this main road," I insist. "Someplace where we can see the bus returning, but where we'll be out of sight." I pull Jing up a sloped side street and into the recessed doorway of a closed shop. Kai follows quickly, Li still coughing in his arms.

It's shady and cool in the doorway, despite the late morning heat. Kai kneels. "Come on, Li," he says, sliding his brother onto the ground. "My shoulder's killing me. It's nicer in here. You got overheated, that's all."

Jing takes the wallet from her pants and opens it. Now that the man and his son are gone, the only question I have is how much money we'll find inside. We'll divide everything up, including the forty yuan. The money will take us to freedom.

Inside the wallet are many, many cards, and Jing quickly sifts through them—credit cards, bank cards, cards I've never seen before. There's a zippered pocket filled with coins that don't add up to much. Jing pulls out the bills and I eagerly watch her count them. I can almost smell the rice fields back home.

Five, ten, twenty, sixty. Kai curses and Jing sits back on her heels and stares at the sky. That will barely buy us anything. All that trouble for sixty yuan?

Kai curses again, louder this time. He takes the wallet from Jing and dumps the coins on the store's doorstep. Then he looks around quickly before darting across the street and tossing the wallet, still filled with its cards, into a trash can.

"What a waste," he mumbles when he returns. "With Yuming's money, we now have, what, one hundred yuan?" He kicks the curb in anger, then goes back to his brother, who is slumped against the door. "Get up, Li," Kai says, nudging him.

Li doesn't move. I peer down the street again, checking for a yellow Windbreaker, Mr. Zhang's predator eyes, and then I turn my attention to Li. He does not look well. I put my fingers on his neck—the way Wai Po used to do to me sometimes—and snap my hand back quickly. His skin is so, so hot. "Li?" I say.

He doesn't respond. His breathing is ragged.

"Li," Kai says, "sit up. You're going to have to get through this if we want to eat again today."

Jing stares at me, then strokes Li's forehead. "Look," she says, "he's shivering."

"He'll be fine," Kai says, annoyed. "He probably went and got a lung infection again. He had one before."

"A lung infection?" I ask, my heart thudding. Like what killed Wai Gong? I drove him, on his tractor, to the clinic in the closest town. He could barely walk, and his body burned with fever. A doctor listened to his heart as Wai Gong lay back, wheezing, on a cot in the one-room building, flies buzzing overhead.

"He'll be fine," Kai says again, snapping me out of my memory.

I swallow hard and glance around. In the park across from the square, bright kites fly, and crowds of tourists move in clumps. White-and-green taxis line the street to the right of the park, waiting for customers. Mr. Zhang could be anywhere. Li coughs again—a dry, painful sound.

Down the main road, to our right, our bus is slowly making its way through the crowds of tourists in the street. "The bus is coming," I tell Jing quietly, looking at Li. His breathing is quick and shallow now, as if each breath is not drawing nearly enough air.

"So go," Kai says, sounding nonchalant and annoyed all at once. "We'll be fine."

"What will you do about Li?" I ask.

"I'm sure his fever will break soon. I'll leave him here, and go get some food and water. Nobody will bother him."

"Leave him?" Jing asks anxiously. "Here in this doorway? Sick? And with Mr. Zhang possibly still searching for us?"

"Look," Kai snaps, "when you live on the streets, you do what you need to do to survive."

"To survive," I repeat, glancing back up the street at the creeping bus. The driver is honking at the surrounding traffic. "But what if . . ." I can't say it. I think of Wai Gong's ashen face in the bed at the clinic. He had seemed better when he went to sleep back home that evening; the doctor had *told* me that the medication would help him. I didn't know. I didn't know that when I pulled the covers around him at bedtime and kissed his hot cheek that by morning he would—

"He'll be fine," Kai says again in a rush. "Like I said, he's had a lung infection before."

In the morning, Wai Gong's body was cold and hard. "But won't he need medicine?" I whisper.

Kai rolls his eyes as Li starts to cough again. He's shivering uncontrollably now, and I look around for something—anything—to cover him with, but there's nothing in sight. I pull off the oversize red T-shirt covering my white one and drape it over Li's torso.

"Your bus is almost here," Kai says over the sound of Li gasping for air. "You better go get it."

I feel like slapping Kai, bringing tears to his sharp, glistening eyes. "While you do what? Stand by and watch your brother suffer, unable to breathe or move? He could *die*."

"I do what I can," Kai spits.

"He needs help," I plead. "My Wai Gong—he had a lung infection. He—he—"

"Your bus has arrived," Kai says, jerking his head toward the main street.

Jing stands with her hands on her hips. "You're not going to get him help, then?" she asks Kai. "A clinic . . ."

"He doesn't need help," Kai insists. "The streets have made our bodies strong. And, besides, help costs *money*."

Down on the main street, the bus doors open. A paper sign for Yetu Village is now taped in the front window. A few people climb aboard. I look again at Li, his tiny, too-thin body shivering, his black hair slicked to the side of his face, every breath shallow. "Well, you can't just do *nothing*," I say, panicked.

"Your bus will leave you if you don't run," Kai replies coldly.

Jing looks back and forth from the bus to Li's shivering body. "There will be other buses," she says to me gently.

I nod. "We could use some of the money for a cab. This is a big town—there will be a hospital."

For the first time, Kai is silent. "And the hospital payment?" he finally asks weakly.

"We'll figure it out," I say, grabbing the money from Kai and bolting down toward the taxis. I glance around frantically as I run, the sound of Li's wheezing cough following me. At the bus stop, the doors to my bus close before me. Jing and I could have been safe now, preparing to speed toward Yetu Village, where Mr. Zhang would never find us. Now we'll spend a good portion of our money to get Li to the hospital, and then Jing and I will have to remain in this town—where Mr. Zhang could be just steps behind us—until we can somehow find a way to get to Shanghai.

But we have no choice, and the hospital—that seems safe enough. Mr. Zhang won't come looking for us there. And maybe, just maybe there will be someone who appears trustworthy enough to not involve the police. We could tell them our story.

From up on the hill, I hear the sound of vomiting. I cringe. "Hurry, Yuming!" Kai shouts. The line of green-and-white taxis stands waiting, their engines idling. I hear Li retching again. The sound makes me nauseous. "He cannot breathe!" Kai screams again, and I stumble. Without even looking around, I dart across the street.

Chapter 26
July 8th
Sunma, Hebei Province, China

Clara

LOLA'S DRAGON KITE was *exactly* like this one, only pink. I was better at flying kites than she was, because I had more patience. Lola didn't like how long it took to get the kite up— having to wait for the wind, then running with the kite for a while until it was *ready* to take off. But I like helping the kite; I like feeling connected to it.

In Shanghai, my kite was a koi fish. Lola and I ran side by side as I shouted instructions to her. *Unroll the string a little more! A little more!* Slowly, slowly, our kites climbed up and up and up until they were sailing and jerking along with hundreds of other bright specks against the sky. Thinking of that koi fish kite reminds me of the baby by the pond at the temple, and how Lola skipped off to play hide-and-seek. I didn't want to play, and she shouldn't have left me alone like that. She *never* should have done that.

Mom and Dad haven't come out of the hotel yet. I'm staying at the near end of the park, where they'll be able to see me as soon as they do. I unwind the string a little and jog with the kite. The wind is perfect and the dragon catches a gust quickly, so I let it rise as I unroll the thin, translucent thread.

In Shanghai, my kite and Lola's had bounced into each other in the air. We'd tried to separate them, but it was hard to do because it was such a windy day; the gusts kept forcing them back together. Eventually, their strings got tangled and they both plummeted to the ground.

Now, I don't have to worry about any of that, because my kite is the only one on this side of the park, rising higher and higher into the blue sky. The dragon—a symbol of luck—dips and drops and climbs. I've already let out probably half of the string.

In the center of the park, families, little kids, and even old people are all flying kites now. It's like the world is upside down and I'm looking down into an ocean full of fish, instead of up at the sky. In the middle of the clump, I see a pink dragon. It looks just like Lola's, and I inch closer to the crowd, letting more and more of my kite line out.

I don't imagine that Lola is at the other end of that string. Instead, I imagine Yuming. *I found your note!* I'd tell her. *I was coming for you!* She would say, *I escaped! I escaped from the factory and now I'm alone.* We would hug each other, like two puzzle pieces fitting together. Mom and Dad would run over. At first they'd be angry with me for taking off, but once they saw that I'd found Yuming, they'd hug her, too.

The pink kite suddenly looks like it's going to drop out of the sky. After I'd yelled out instructions to Lola at the kite festival in Shanghai, she'd asked me, *Now what? Now what, Clara?* I make my way closer to the dragon.

I'm in the center of the park, surrounded by people and kite strings. I trip over a tree root and almost fall. The shock of it makes me feel like crying. I see the Chinese girl who told us about the gondola. She waves and smiles up at the blue dragon her uncle sold me. I wave back. The pink dragon is moving farther away, and I follow it until I'm at the other end of the park, near a row of green-and-white taxis on a side street.

The pink dragon is just overhead now. I run toward it, looking up, until my blue one is right next to it. I tug my string and draw it in a bit until the two dragons are sailing side by side. I keep pretending that Yuming is controlling the pink kite, and I even tug on my string until the blue dragon bumps up against the pink one. *Hey!* I picture Yuming yelling to me, laughing. *Watch it!*

"Hey!" a little boy near me yells. He looks like he's six or seven. "Someone's trying to take my kite down!" he says to his dad in a British accent. "Who's got the blue dragon?" He looks around, but I don't say anything. I try to look innocent and turn my head toward the taxis.

I see a Chinese kid run to one of the cabs, say something to the driver, and shove a wad of money into his hand before jumping into the backseat.

My parents told me never to show my money in public, because it could attract pickpockets. I keep my wallet in my backpack.

I look back up at the kites—the pink dragon and the blue dragon. They're bouncing off each other. I'm surrounded by cheering families and little kids running in circles, staring with wonder at their kites overhead. I stand there in the middle of it all, just watching.

"Hey! Hey! Who has the blue dragon?" the British boy calls out again. "It's in trouble."

Without realizing it, I dropped my kite handle. It is skittering away from me across the grass. For a minute, my dragon just hovers, still attracted somehow to the pink one next to it. Then, the boy jerks his kite away from mine and my dragon flies up and up and up, whipping around this way and that. The handle is way out of my reach now. The kite floats over the trees until a gust of wind catches it, jerking it upward. I watch it get smaller and smaller, until it's just a blue speck in front of the mountains. Then it's gone. I look at the place where the blue dot used to be—the place where there used to be something, and now there's nothing—and I don't understand how it's possible for a thing to exist one second and vanish the next.

My eyes wander over to the cabs again. It wouldn't do any harm to see—just *see* if any of the drivers know the way to the pink factory. I mean, it's so close, and Yuming needs help; *all* those kids need help. It's too late for Lola, but with Yuming, it's different. With Yuming, there's still some hope.

Slowly, I walk toward the first cab in the long line, the British boy calling after me, "Hey, why'd you let go of your kite?"

I don't answer. I lean into the window of the cab.

"Do you speak English?" I ask the driver. He shrugs.

I try the next cab in the line. "English?"

"Yes," the driver says. "Speak English."

"Do you know of a pink factory?"

"Factory, yes."

"A pink one," I say, trying not to cry.

"Pink?" the driver asks slowly, like he's thinking. I watch him, my heart thudding. "Yes, pink. I know pink factory." He points out the window. "That direction. Make clothing there. Make many things."

I nod. "Yes!"

"Yes," the driver says, looking confused. "I can take you. But why—"

I yank the car door open and quickly jump inside, ignoring his question.

"You have money?" the driver asks suspiciously, studying me in the rearview mirror.

I unzip the inside pocket of my backpack with shaking hands and pull out the money that Mom and Dad gave me in case of an emergency—three hundred yuan. I hold it up for him to see.

He nods, still studying me like he doesn't trust me, before finally pulling carefully onto the street. He honks at the crowd—the families and tourists, the angry-looking man in a yellow Windbreaker—and I think of Mom and Dad. They're going to *kill* me.

The driver honks once more before looking back at me again in the rearview mirror. "It is very crowded right now in Sunma," he explains. His face is lined with deep wrinkles and his black hair is streaked with gray. "Many people."

I nod and look out the window at the British boy, who is holding his kite and watching me, his dad by his side. When the crowd finally passes, we pull forward onto the main road.

I press my forehead to the window and stare at the kites flying over the park, at the gondola station, and, finally, at the tiny, run-down storefronts. The driver makes his way carefully around the potholes in the gravel road and soon Sunma becomes nothing but white buildings, the red temple and bright-green hills behind me.

I lean back, study the gray ceiling of the cab, and exhale slowly. I can't believe I'm doing it— I'm so close to tracking down what might really be Yuming's factory. Lola would be so proud.

I feel bad for not waiting for Mom and Dad—when they can't find me near the hotel, they'll freak out—but right now, doing this is the most important thing.

Maybe this is how it was with Lola at the temple two years ago. She must have known that day that I would be scared of losing her, but when she saw the baby and her parents at the pond, she had to go watch them. Sometimes there are things you just *have* to do.

The cab climbs slowly up a winding mountain road. Trees jut out of the mountainside; I could touch them if I opened the window all the way. Instead, I pull out my map—the one the other cabdriver gave to me—and try to figure out where we are.

"I see you have map," the driver says to me, making conversation. He seems like a nice guy, and I'll be sure to point out to Mom and Dad later, when I'm in huge trouble, that he definitely wasn't the type to kidnap some random tourist from America.

I nod. "Yeah."

"The street we take is called 52," he explains, gesturing out his open window to a gray stretch of road up ahead. At a tiny intersection there's a sign with the number 52 on it, and we turn left. The road dips down, into a valley.

"My village is just that way," he says, pointing to his right. I turn my map to the side and find where we are. We're heading northeast on 52, out of Sunma. The road becomes bumpier beneath us.

The driver stops at another small intersection and looks around. "I think . . ." he says, as though talking to himself, "I think we turn there." He points left, hesitating.

"Do you need this?" I ask him, handing my map forward.

"Ah, thank you." He studies it, turns it around, and studies it some more. "Right," he says. "We turn right." He hands it back to me. "Good thing we have map."

"I don't need it anymore. You can keep it," I tell him.

"Keep it?"

I nod and pull Yuming's photograph out of my pocket as the cab turns right onto another pitted road. A pickup truck passes us. It's carrying a load of chickens, and a wispy white feather floats into my open window. There's a little girl with pigtails sitting alone in the back of the pickup. She gets smaller and smaller until she disappears from sight.

"So," the driver calls back, over the roar of the wind, "why an American girl like you go to factory?"

It seems like a simple question, but I feel embarrassed answering it. I shrug, and he smiles back at me. "You forget?" he jokes. Then his face turns serious. "Your father know where you are?"

I ignore his last question and hold up Yuming's photograph. It flutters wildly in the wind. He holds out his hand, and I pass it to him. He glances down at it quickly, then back up to the road. "You know this family?" he asks skeptically.

"Sort of," I say.

"Southern family," he adds.

"How do you know?"

"Easy to tell," he answers quickly. "Rice farmers, most likely."

"The girl?" I say suddenly. "She's trapped in the pink factory and . . ." I look down at the feather in my hand and then up at the back of the driver's head. "She needs me. I'm going to help her."

It sounds ridiculous when I say the words out loud, and for some reason I flash to Lola in her hospital bed, her head bald, her skin pale and laced with blue veins. I hold the feather out the open window and let the wind yank it away. What would Lola have said—not the Lola with long black hair who I keep imagining, but the *real* Lola—if I had whispered to her while she was dying that I was going to go to China to try to save another girl because I couldn't save *her*?

At the very end, Lola didn't look like herself; I could barely even recognize her. Mom would carefully slide the hats that Grandma Betty had knitted for her onto her bald head. They were so stupid, and Lola would have hated them if she could have seen herself in them, but by then, she hardly ever opened her eyes. Her face was puffy, and sometimes I'd stare at her from across the hospital room and pretend she was someone else—someone I didn't know, not my sister. It wasn't hard to do.

"Trapped? Help her?" The cab is slowing down.

"She doesn't have any family. We were thinking about . . . I mean, *I* was thinking of asking her if . . ."

I think of the oxygen machine Lola was hooked up to at the end, with the mask she kept trying to pull off in her sleep.

The driver holds the photograph up for me to take, and I look down at Yuming's smiling face. At the end, Lola had dark, puffy circles under her eyes—her eyes that were almost always closed. I'd say her name, but she wouldn't answer.

"I wanted to see if she wanted to come home with us," I finish.

"Southern farming girl come home with you? To America?"

I don't say anything. I just look out the window at the tiny village to our left and the slanted, pitted road leading up to the pale-pink factory.

When I'd leave the hospital room, which was only when Mom and Dad would drag me outside for some fresh air, I'd miss the awful smell of it: the rubbing alcohol, the bleach.

"How would this girl come home with you?" The driver has stopped the cab in the middle of the road.

"I don't know," I whisper. I don't even know if he can hear me.

When Lola died, I was relieved. I was relieved because I could picture her the way she used to be again—the way she was *supposed* to be.

Up ahead, the bright-orange sun is just starting to set in a fiery ball beside the factory. I look down one more time at the photograph of Yuming—the girl I wanted to replace Lola with—and I start to cry. "I wanted her to be part of my family."

The driver turns to face me completely. "Her life is here. I think better idea is go back to kite festival now," he says gently. "Your family at park?"

I nod and look up at him, away from the picture of Yuming. Yes. My family is at the park.

Chapter 27

Yuming

THE SOUNDS OF the hospital surround us and they bring to mind the never-ending *chug, chug, chug* of the sewing machines. Doors swoosh open and shut. A young man moans, a rag pressed to his bleeding forehead. A baby cries. Li is slumped over Kai's shoulder, his lips tinted purple. I turn in a circle, surveying our surroundings, trying to figure out what to do.

"Over there, I think," Jing says, pointing to a long line at the front of the room. She races over to secure a spot as Kai and I follow, monitoring Li's shallow breathing. Memories of Wai Gong pound against my mind, begging to be let in, but I will not allow it. Not now.

The line creeps forward the way Wai Po walked near the end of her life, when every step and every breath caused her pain. Jing gnaws at her fingernails. I keep my hand in front of

Li's mouth, feeling for his faint breath. Kai stares straight ahead as he holds his brother, a dazed look on his face. He does not say a word.

At last it is our turn to talk to the woman behind the counter. She looks us over. She does not ask for the patient's name and birth date as she did of the man who was in line right before us. For a long moment, she stares at us. Then she clears her throat. "Where are the patient's parents?" she asks curtly.

Kai opens his mouth to speak, but nothing comes out.

"They are working," I say quickly.

The woman shakes her head. "We cannot admit a child without a parent present."

As if struck by lightning, Kai cries out, "But he has a lung infection! He cannot breathe! He could die!"

She is silent for a moment. She clears her throat again. "Besides, payment is required up front. Do you have money?"

"How much do we have left?" Kai asks desperately, shifting Li's weight.

I empty my pockets onto the countertop. Fourteen yuan. I look down, ashamed.

"We cannot admit a patient before payment is collected," she tells us.

"Please!" Kai yells. Several people in the waiting room are watching us now.

The woman stands up. I think she is going to push us out the door. Instead, she says, "Stay here. I will ask my supervisor," before disappearing through a doorway to her right.

I take a deep breath as Kai rests Li's bottom on the desk. His cheek is still plastered to his brother's shoulder, his face sweaty and flushed, his breathing quick wheezes.

The woman finally returns and takes her seat before us. "My supervisor is asking the department chair if he will see you. Please step to the side." Jing, Kai, and I exchange glances before Kai lifts Li, and we move to the right. The next patient, a young lady with a blood-soaked bandage wrapped around her hand, steps forward.

Time passes. Kai gently places Li on the floor, his head resting in Jing's lap. I sit beside his feet, my hand on his burning ankle and watch the red electronic numbers change on the sign on the wall. 52, 53, 54. We don't even have a number yet. Li grunts as if he is trying to cough but doesn't have the energy. 68, 69, 70. I close my eyes. I try not to see Wai Gong. You are doing fine, I tell myself. I open my eyes. Kai lies down next to his brother, his hand on Li's chest to keep track of the faint rhythm of his breathing. 89, 90, 91. The double doors open.

"They're on the floor right here," the woman says.

Kai jumps up and cries, "My brother!" before I even have time to stand. Two men stand before us. One wears a white coat with SUPERVISOR embroidered on the front pocket. The other, in a navy suit, has a name tag around his neck that reads HOSPITAL PRESIDENT. I know Jing and Kai cannot read these labels.

"Sir," I say directly to the president, "he cannot breathe. He will die. We will find some way to pay you later—"

The president squints at me and purses his lips, as if thinking.

He squats beside Li, placing his hand on the boy's cheek and then over his tiny, barely moving chest before standing back up.

He looks from me to Kai to Jing. "Payment will not be necessary," he finally states, turning to the supervisor. "Take them to the fever ward."

The supervisor nods. "Yes, sir."

I want to laugh and cry all at once, I am so relieved. Jing gently pushes Li's torso upward to Kai, who hefts his brother over his shoulder again.

"Thank you," we all say almost in unison to the hospital president. "Thank you."

He smiles kindly at us before disappearing back through the double doorway.

Jing, Kai, and I exchange looks of triumph as we follow the supervisor into an elevator, down a hallway, and into a large, crowded hospital room with a sign reading FEVER WARD over the doorway.

In the back corner, the supervising doctor parts the curtains of an enclosure and motions to the empty bed. Kai places Li carefully on the white sheet. A nurse joins us and the hospital president reappears, pushing one wooden chair toward us and pulling another. A second nurse follows him, carrying a third chair.

The first nurse waits until the chairs are pushed against the back wall before unlocking the wheels on Li's bed and rolling him toward the doorway. "He will need a chest X-ray," she states. Kai looks like he wants to protest, but Jing takes his arm and pulls him to one of the chairs where he slumps, exhausted.

Now, several hours later, Li is breathing evenly. His lips are pink once again. An IV drips medication into his vein, an oxygen mask rests over his tiny face, and a plastic hospital bracelet is secured around his thin wrist. Doctors come and go, paying little attention to Jing, Kai, and me, and a new worry takes shape: the police. Surely the hospital president will have to contact the police to deal with the four children who, clearly, are homeless.

I glance at Jing and Kai, suddenly panicked once again—and so, so tired. I picture the police storming into the hospital, Mr. Zhang behind them. *These are my nieces, these are my nephews, they are mine.* He'll shove us into a car and drive us back to the factory. The days ahead will stretch into a gray forever until I become a woman with dead eyes.

"Kai? Jing?" I ask. "The Sunma police—could they be on Mr. Zhang's side, too?

"I don't know," Jing says. She stands up, walks over to Li's sleeping body, and strokes his hand before glancing around the small, curtained enclosure. She looks as if she is torn between wanting to bolt and wanting to stay.

Kai, who seems defeated, just shrugs.

"You always have an answer to this type of question," I say to him, trying to urge him out of his fog of shock and exhaustion. "You're the expert!"

He just shakes his head. His quiet makes me uneasy; it makes me feel as if we have already parted ways.

The curtains open. Several doctors, including the hospital president, enter the enclosure. The generous president, who likely saved Li's life, smiles our way. I wonder if he has called the police yet.

The other doctors don't acknowledge us, but instead crowd around Li's hospital bed in a semicircle. "This is an approximately seven-year-old male," one of them says to the others. "He was brought in with oxygen deprivation, cough, fever, and loss of consciousness. The X-ray confirmed pneumonia, and he will be on an intravenous antibiotic for ten days."

Kai squeezes his eyes shut—perhaps in disbelief, perhaps in relief, perhaps in an attempt to block everything out. When he opens them, they are rimmed with pink. He stares down at the tiled floor.

I know what I need to do.

The president looks on from the foot of Li's bed. Shakily, I get up from the wooden chair that he so considerately dragged into the room for me. My heart is chugging and my veins are flooding, yet again, with fear. There too many *what-if*s in this life that cannot be my life any longer.

I move next to the president. The right pocket of his expensive navy suit jacket is heavy with his wallet. I glance around the bed, recalling Kai's words on the bus: *Distract him, engage his compassion.*

I will pay you back. Forgive me.

"Sir?" I say, looking down at my filthy shoes. Out of the corner of my eye, I see Kai raise his head. "His feet appeared swollen when we brought him in."

Jing leaps up and joins me. "Yes, they were," she confirms, as if reading my mind.

A tiny smile appears on Kai's lips—so tiny it is almost not there.

"Could you take a look?" I ask.

The hospital president steps closer to Li, lifts the white sheet off of his tiny, mud-caked feet, and examines them. Jing and I take a step closer, crowding him.

After the next harvest, I will send money.

"They do not appear swollen," the hospital president says.

"Underneath," I say quietly, pressing closer still. His suit smells like wool—like Wai Gong's good jacket that still hangs on a hook in the corner, back home.

He bends to peer at the underside of Li's feet. Jing and I bend, too. I look at Li's feet—calloused by his hard life—and stroke them gently with my right hand. "Just there, near the underside of the toes," I lie. "It was swollen there earlier."

Forgive me. Please, please forgive me.

"Well, they look fine now," the president announces, smiling warmly at me and then Jing. "We will keep an eye on them."

"Thank you, sir," we both say again and again. "Thank you for everything."

The president leads the doctors out of the room, closing the curtains behind them. When they are gone, I pull the sheet carefully back over Li's feet.

Kai nods at us as though he has come, at least partially, back to life. "Well done, Princess," he whispers proudly to me. Jing squats next to Li's bed and pulls the thick, black wallet out from where I had tossed it onto the floor. I pretend not to notice when Kai wipes tears from his eyes.

He clears his throat. "Hurry. You won't have long," he whispers. "Take only what you think you'll need."

Jing opens the wallet. Inside, there's a large wad of cash, and she sifts through it before pulling out a bit more than half. Kai glances at the closed curtains, over to Li, and then back to Jing and me. "Split that between the two of you," he whispers quickly, "in case you get separated. Keep it in your front pants pockets only. Make a plan, a meeting spot for every city you stop in, just in case. Here, give me the wallet."

He rifles through the cards and pulls out a bus pass. "This probably has money on it. Maybe you won't have to pay to get to the train station."

Behind us, Li's oxygen mask hums and he stirs in his sleep. "You'd better go," Kai says. "The doctor will realize this is missing soon—any second." He crouches down and tucks the wallet back onto the floor under Li's bed. "He'll find it here, and suspect us. I'll let him search me. He'll see I don't have the money. But he'll know you took it."

Fear has made my mouth dry. For a moment, I cannot speak. I hug Kai tightly. "If Mr. Zhang doesn't get you first, they'll send Li to an orphanage," I eventually whisper.

I feel him shrug. "It doesn't matter," he whispers back. I take a step away from him and see that he's finally smiling again. "If that happens, he'll grab a hot meal there and escape. We'll be back on the streets in no time."

I laugh a little, because I know what he says is true. "When we get far enough south, we'll tell the police about the factory," I promise him. "If you end up back there, it won't be for long. We'll make them listen—somehow, we'll make them do something."

Kai nods.

"Thank you," I say. "Thank you for getting us out of the factory."

"Thank you for saving my brother. I wouldn't have brought him here."

I walk over to Li and stroke his grimy hair as Jing hugs Kai silently for a long time. She takes off the thin knapsack she has been carrying since we escaped from the factory and hands it to him. "The scissors," she says. "They're inside. You might need them." She wipes her cheeks, wet with tears. "When he seems well enough, cut off his hospital bracelet and get out—maybe you can escape before the police are called."

Kai, wiping his own eyes again, takes the knapsack from Jing.

I wrap my arms around his neck. "Thank you," I whisper again. It's all I can come up with. Kai takes a step back. We all know that the president will return soon, looking for his wallet. I take Jing's arm. She bends quickly and kisses Li's cheek. "Tell him good-bye for us?" I ask Kai.

He nods, his lips tight with sadness, worry, and fatigue.

With one last look at Kai and Li, the boys who helped us

escape the factory, we slip through the doorway and out the main doors of the hospital into the cool night air.

☆

After all we have been through, the journey to the train station seems almost *too* easy. We board a bus outside the hospital, sliding the doctor's pass through the slot twice. We sit in clean seats as the bus rumbles past the center of town, which is still crowded with kite festival tourists, despite the late hour. The small train station is cool with air conditioning and bustling with people coming and going from the festival. We feel safer in their midst; they make it feel less likely that we will be spotted by anyone who might be looking for us. We make our way cautiously to the ticket window, where I ask for two one-way tickets to Shanghai.

"You'll need to switch trains in Beijing," the ticket seller tells me. "If you rush when you get to the station, you'll be able to make the train that departs ten minutes after yours arrives."

I nod. Jing takes the money from her front pants pocket. We have more than enough.

"Hard seats or soft seats?" the woman behind the window asks.

I look at Jing. Soft seats will cost more, but I can just imagine it: the two of us leaning back on cushions as we speed away from the north and our fear of Mr. Zhang—as we speed away from everything about this life. We deserve a comfortable sleep, Wai Gong, I think.

Jing smiles a little and nods, as if reading my mind again.

"Soft, please," I whisper, silently thanking the president of the hospital and promising, once again, to pay him back.

The next train leaves in less than twenty minutes. Jing and I make our way toward the boarding platform. There are several shops within the station and, still checking over our shoulders for Mr. Zhang and the police, we stop to buy the first packaged food we see and two matching blue sweatshirts. We tug the shirts over our heads and hurry to the platform, where we show our tickets to a man in uniform. "Good timing—only a few seats left," he tells us, directing us onto the nearly full train car. We sink, side by side, into large, comfortable seats at the back. There is only a little window, but we don't care. We've seen enough.

In four minutes, this train will depart for Beijing Station. Once there, we'll rush onto the first-class car of our next train, using the tickets we've already purchased, and continue the overnight journey to Shanghai. I can smell the sea, now just eight hours away. I can visualize the ride inland by bus—to my rice fields and small, cozy house. They float in front of me, already welcoming me home.

Chapter 28

Clara

EVEN THOUGH IT'S almost ten o'clock at night, the Sunma Village train station is crowded with tourists coming and going from the kite festival. I hold tightly to Mom's hand as we make our way through the crowd. Faces swim in front of me, and I feel like I'm sleepwalking, like the day we left the hospital for the last time on the morning after Lola died. My hand is wrapped around her ashes in my pocket.

Dad walks to the ticket window while Mom and I stand off to the side. I watch him squint up at the illuminated departure schedule, then back at the woman in the booth. Even though Mom and Dad are right here with me, I feel alone—just like after Lola died and before I found Yuming's note and picture in the purse at Bellman's.

Dad comes back, three tickets to Beijing in hand, his fore-head wrinkled and his shoulders slumped in exhaustion. I know he's furious with me—he and Mom both are. Right now they probably think I'm way more of a wreck about Lola dying than they ever could have imagined, but the truth is that I'm starting to get used to this—this feeling of being on my own.

Neither of them has said anything about punishment yet; all they've done is hug me and ask me if I'm okay. Mom won't let go of my hand, as though she's worried I'm going to run off again. I guess there's no way she could know that I understand now that there's no point.

When the cabdriver pulled up at the taxi stand at the park, Dad was already talking frantically with three police officers and the British boy's father. Mom was on hold with the United States Embassy. The cabdriver walked me over to them and told them *everything*.

☆

Now I pull my sweatshirt out of my backpack as we walk toward the waiting trains. It's freezing in the train station. Mom points us to Platform Seven. Tourists walk around with kites, bags, and tickets in hand. Most are probably returning to Beijing, just like us.

The train waits at the platform, a conductor standing in front of the door to the first-class car. It looks crowded inside, and Dad pushes ahead to check it out. "I'll just see how many seats they have left," he says. "It looks pretty full. There's another train in twenty minutes."

"'Kay, we'll be right here," Mom calls to him as he disappears into the crowd. I don't say anything.

If it were before—even earlier in the day today—I would have imagined Lola standing with us. I'd picture her bouncing up and down, her black hair swinging. *You were so close!* I'd hear her saying. *You almost did it! Don't give up now!*

But I don't see or hear her. She's not here anymore.

Dad had sent Susan Zhau an email while we were in the cab to the train station. He told her we were in Sunma, north of Beijing, and that we'd spotted a pink factory from a gondola. He didn't mention anything about how close I had gotten to it.

"Everything all right now?" I hear from behind me. Mom and I turn around.

"Oh, hi," I say, embarrassed. It's the British man from the park. Next to him is another man holding the little boy, who is asleep on his shoulder.

"We just have to thank you again," Mom says as I look at my feet. Seeing the little boy makes me think of his pink dragon kite—and Lola's. I wish I could only remember the good times, how she was when she was healthy. But I can't. I know I can't do that.

"Of course," the man says. "I'm just glad everything ended well."

"I don't know what we would have done if you hadn't seen Clara get into that cab. . . ." Mom goes on.

I'm so exhausted I feel like I'm floating underwater—like all of China is underwater, the way I pictured it when I was younger and Lola and I tried to dig our way here in our sandbox. I wish I could dig a hole now and disappear while Mom and the two men talk. They'll never understand why I did what I did, and I don't have the energy to explain.

"Elise! Clara!" Dad calls from behind us. I turn around. He's beckoning to us from next to the conductor.

"Well, we'd better run," Mom says to the man and his family. "Thank you again."

Just before we reach Dad, a Chinese couple with a young daughter hand their tickets to the conductor and slide into the last open seats in the car. The little girl kneels on her seat to look over its back, and she makes a funny face at two Chinese girls about my age. Their faces look golden and wavy through the tinted window.

Dad watches her, too. One of the girls in the seat behind her makes a face back at her, and the little girl grins before turning around and plopping down next to her mom. "That little girl reminds me of Lola," Dad says, still looking through the tinted train window.

"Yeah," I say, nodding, "everything reminds me of Lola."

"We'll get the next train," he says, putting his arm around me and pulling me closer to him. I nod again as the doors swish shut and the train pulls out of the station.

☆

The next night, we take the overnight train from Beijing to Shanghai Station. We arrive early in the morning and make the easy walk to the fancy hotel we stayed in the last time we were in Shanghai. It's right across the street from Lola's park.

We ride the elevator up to the sixth floor, and as my parents check out the hotel room for non-functioning lights and drainless tubs, I walk to the window, part the curtains, and look down at Lola's fountain. The water sparkles in the early morning light.

Mom comes to stand behind me and rests her chin on the top of my head, not saying anything.

"Hey!" Dad calls. He's sitting on the edge of the bed, looking at his phone. "Listen to this! 'Dear Mr. Clay,' he starts to read. 'Thank you for your recent email inquiring after the factory in Hebei Province. Chinese authorities have located a factory fitting the description in the note and have launched an investigation. We will continue to keep you informed. Sincerely, Susan Zhau.'"

"Wow," Mom says, sitting down next to Dad to look at his phone.

"Amazing," Dad says as Mom reads it again. "I could have sworn that she was going to blow us off."

I press my forehead against the window. I can't believe it. Maybe giving that note to Susan Zhau actually *did* help save Yuming and the other kids in the factory after all.

I turn around. "Dad? Mom?" I say. "I think I'm going to walk across to Lola's park."

Mom hands Dad his phone and jumps up off the bed. "Give me a sec, honey. I'll come with you."

I need to go alone, but I don't blame them for not trusting me—not after what I did in Sunma two days ago. "Would you mind just watching me from the window?" I ask. "I have to do something. By myself." When I see their faces go pale, I add, "I promise I won't do anything crazy this time."

Mom sits back down slowly and nods as I walk out the door toward the elevator.

Outside of the hotel, the sky is white and there's a cool breeze. The light angles toward me from the park. I cross the quiet street, turn around, and look up. Mom and Dad wave to me from the window.

The park smells like wet earth and also the ocean, which is just a few blocks away. I walk along the cracked cement path that leads to Lola's fountain—to Yuming's fountain—and I look at the semicircle of willow trees behind it. I think of Lola when she was a baby in the narrow cardboard box before she was even my sister. I can't believe all that had to happen to bring us together—how her birth mother couldn't take care of her and brought her to this park, how someone took her to the orphanage nearby, how my parents wanted to adopt . . . So many things could have turned out differently, and then I wouldn't have known her—I never would have known my sister.

I take the small silver box of Lola's ashes out of my pocket and, for the first time, I unscrew the top. The ashes are grayish white and, when I touch them, they're softer than I expected them to be. It seems so wrong and so impossible that a person could disappear, just like that—that a person could be your sister one minute and ashes in a silver box the next.

The stone tiers of the fountain shine under a coat of dew. The drops are sparkling like glitter—like tiny drops of life—and I step closer to the edge. I stand in the spot where Lola was found almost fourteen years ago, and I think about all the layers of living that are always passing over and under one another like threads in a tapestry.

There's a splashing sound in front of me. I look up. Standing on the edge of the fountain is a little Chinese girl. She's barefoot and translucent, like a spirit, and she's smiling at me, her long black hair blowing across her face. She's wearing an impossibly tiny yellow T-shirt with a faded rainbow on it and blue jeans that are too short on her, and she squats down to touch the water, as though she's testing whether it's too cold to swim in. When she stands back up, she tucks her hair behind her ears and studies me. I can see her small chest moving up and down as she breathes, and I want to reach out for her, but I know I can't.

She sticks her tongue out at me and, grinning, jumps down from the ledge of the fountain onto the cement path. She pushes her stringy black hair off her face again and waves. I don't want her to go, but I can only watch her walk away toward the willow trees, even though she's way too young to be on her own. She becomes more and more translucent until she finally disappears completely.

Then, slowly and carefully, I tip her ashes into her fountain. For a minute, they float on the surface—a grayish-white, dusty blob—but then they drown quickly in a clump. They fade into the water, and I put the empty box back into my pocket.

The early morning sun seeps through the clouds and breaks over the tips of the willow trees, and I look at the tiny dewdrops on the grass and the leaves around me. They remind me of Lola—of how she's nowhere and everywhere, all at the same time.

Then I take out Yuming's photograph—the photograph that I still can't believe was taken right here, in this very spot. If it weren't for Yuming, I wouldn't have come back to China; I wouldn't be here *right now*. I look one more time at the easy smile of the girl with long black hair—hair just like Lola *used to* have. I look at her brother and her grandparents, and I'm happy, because if what Susan Zhau said is true, then I really think Yuming is going to be okay.

I pick up a stone by my feet, I turn it over and over in my hands, and I say good-bye. I say good-bye to my sister, and I say good-bye to Yuming, the girl I'd wanted so badly to save all by myself—the girl I'd hoped would fill the black hole.

I put Yuming's photograph on the ledge of the fountain, right above the spot where Lola was found, and I rest the rock on top of it to hold it in place. Then I walk toward the narrow archway that leads out of the park.

When I get to the archway, I step aside to let two girls in matching blue sweatshirts pass by. The way their arms are linked, they remind me of Lola and myself—how we were, and how we could have been—and I wonder if they're sisters. I smile at them. They both smile back, and I cross the street to where Mom and Dad are waiting for me in the hotel doorway.

Chapter 29

September 1st
Yemo Village, China

Yuming

THE NIGHTTIME SOUNDS that float through my window are so familiar. The rustling stalks of the dry rice fields, the hooting owls, even the buzzing of the flying ants. I pay attention to them like I never did before. I breathe in the smells of the open air and hold them close.

The sounds inside the house are even more comforting. The quiet rhythm of Jing's breathing as she sleeps in the bed next to me. Bolin washing our dinner bowls in the other room. The way that he squints at the dishes and wipes them clean with his soapy palm reminds me of Wai Gong. I know that tomorrow morning I'll wake to find him snoring, his head against the clay wall, while sitting in the stiff chair next to the bed.

In the moonlight I can see my framed photograph on the

windowsill. It is speckled with tiny water drops from the spray of the fountain, and there are creases in it, but Wai Po's and Wai Gong's faces are clear and smiling. Sometimes I think I need many, many things, but other times I think I have everything I need right here: Bolin, Jing, and this copy of my photograph.

I think back to when Jing found it, on the day we spent in Shanghai before we took the bus home to Yemo Village. It was after we'd gone to the police about the factory. Maybe Kai was right—maybe the police were never really on Mr. Zhang's side—but I'm still glad we used pretend names when we filed the report. We didn't have any luck when we talked to the street vendors at Molihua Park: None of them knew of Bolin.

But my luck changed at the fountain—at our *lucky fountain*.

We arrived home the following day to find Bolin waiting for us. He had returned to Yemo Village in June to visit and help Wai Gong with the harvest. The crop had been ready for picking, but Bolin had had to do it all himself. I wish I had been here with Bolin to touch what Wai Gong had sowed before he fell ill.

"Your brother harvested rice every morning and drove your Wai Gong's tractor to town to check with the police every afternoon," Mrs. Huang, our neighbor, told me. "While you were gone, he was inconsolable." Min Li, now seven, peeked out from behind her mama's back as we spoke, looking at me as though I were a stranger. Only when I knelt in front of her and let her touch my short hair did she smile, exposing a mouth of newly missing teeth.

☆

The wind gusts, ruffling the trimmed stumps of rice stalks outside the window. Jing is sleeping peacefully, but for me, sleep doesn't come so easily. Too many thoughts tumble in my mind. I try to relax my body one muscle at a time, like Wai Gong taught me.

Sometimes I sing Wai Po's lullaby to myself. Occasionally, I can even hear her voice, soft and raspy.

The moon is bright,
the wind is quiet,
tree leaves hang over your window.
My little baby, go to sleep quickly.
Sleep and dream sweet dreams.

I pull her song up and over me; I wrap it around myself like a blanket. In the morning, the sounds of the birds will replace her song. Bolin will stroll to the park, hands clasped behind his back, and play xiangqi with the men until planting season comes again. Jing and I will walk the path to the school side by side. Wai Po and Wai Gong will be with us, too—in the dewdrops on the grass, in the chalk dust at the schoolhouse, and waiting in the fog over the rice fields when we arrive home in the evening.

Author's Note

ON THE MORNING of April 29, 2014, I spent a long while staring at my blank computer screen. I was feeling unproductive and it seemed like a good time to procrastinate, so I got up from the couch, stood in front of my kitchen window for several minutes, and then scrolled through some news stories online. One caught my eye: an article about an Australian woman in New York who had found a handwritten note and a photograph at the bottom of her shopping bag. The note was a plea for help from an African man in a Chinese factory prison who had made the shopping bag, and the photo was of his face.

The story was haunting for a variety of reasons, not the least of which was this: In every practical and logical sense, the lady in New York would never have known this man—but now, because of the note in the bag, she did. I was struck by the fact that two very different lives in two such disparate parts of the world could become so suddenly intertwined. It felt extremely powerful to me that two lives could be linked by one piece of paper, one photograph, and one brave plea for help. As it turns out, the man was released from the prison before anyone could act on his note, but that didn't detract from the power of the story. Certainly, the outcome was important, but I was focused on the *connection*.

In *Threads*, Clara and Yuming are girls leading completely different lives on opposite sides of the globe. In theory, their paths never should cross. But, just like in the true story of the man in the prison factory and the woman in New York, one piece of paper, one photograph, and one act of bravery bind them together.

I knew that, to write the book I wanted to write, I would need to do a lot of research. China is a vast and complex country, populated by a billion and a half people from many very different cultural groups. I had to read a lot and talk to several people in order to figure out what Yuming's life *might* have looked like. I researched Chinese factories and Chinese thirteen-year-olds, but when it came to putting a thirteen-year-old in a Chinese factory, which is illegal, I had to make some inferences. While I used several actual locations, such as Beijing, Shanghai, and the Great Wall, most of the locations in *Threads* are fictionalized. I needed to create small towns, villages, temples, and parks to meet the needs of the story. There is no pale-pink factory with three of four smokestacks working, no village called Sunma with a gondola. But there are street vendors, bored teenagers on buses, helpful cabdrivers, and diligent rice farmers, all leading separate but interconnected lives.

I am indebted to my neighbor and friend Cindy Bai, who, over many cups of tea and plates of Chinese snacks, answered my seemingly endless questions about her home country. Shannon Moffett kindly answered my many questions about Chinese emergency medicine and provided me with priceless details about the Chinese medical system. Jason Gronkiewicz-Doran generously assisted me with my research. Tammy Polonsky continued to serve as my always-on-call general medical consultant on matters ranging from lung infections to childhood cancer. My mom, Barbara Hurwitz, made the writing of this story possible. Lea Wang vetted the final manuscript and helped me put on the finishing touches. My trusted agent, Wendy Schmalz, protected my creative process, as she always does, and my insightful and talented editor, Stephanie Lurie, made *Threads* infinitely better than it ever could have been without her.

Sometimes I lie in bed at night and think about the fact that my life is, in one way or another, connected to every single other life on the planet. It's as though there are invisible threads that bind us all, and occasionally, when I envision these invisible threads, they feel charged with unseen energy. Every now and then, like in the cases of the man in the factory and the woman in New York, and Clara and Yuming, an invisible thread becomes exposed. The energy creates tangible, visible sparks and, from these sparks, come stories.

Susan Libman

AMI POLONSKY is a reading and writing teacher, the mother of two children, and the author of the critically acclaimed novel *Gracefully Grayson*. She is passionate about guiding children toward a love of books and helping to create lifetime readers. Ami lives outside of Chicago with her family.